W9-CBT-308

4

LARGE PRINT FICTION MACOMBER

Macomber, Debbie
Sugar and spice /

11/14/13

SUGAR AND SPICE

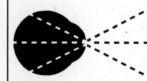

This Large Print Book carries the
Seal of Approval of N.A.V.H.

SUGAR AND SPICE

DEBBIE MACOMBER

THORNDIKE PRESS
A part of Gale, Cengage Learning

GALE
CENGAGE Learning·

Detroit • New York • San Francisco • New Haven, Conn • Waterville, Maine • London

GALE
CENGAGE Learning·

Copyright © 1987 by Debbie Macomber.
Thorndike Press, a part of Gale, Cengage Learning.

ALL RIGHTS RESERVED
This is a work of fiction. Names, characters, places, and incidents are either the product of the author's imagination or are used fictitiously, and any resemblance to actual persons, living or dead, business establishments, events or locales is entirely coincidental.
Thorndike Press® Large Print Romance.
The text of this Large Print edition is unabridged.
Other aspects of the book may vary from the original edition.
Set in 18 pt. Plantin.

LIBRARY OF CONGRESS CATALOGING-IN-PUBLICATION DATA

Macomber, Debbie.
  Sugar and spice / by Debbie Macomber.
    pages ; cm. — (Thorndike Press large print romance)
    ISBN 978-1-4104-5684-7 (hardcover) — ISBN 1-4104-5684-6 (hardcover) 1.
  Large type books. I. Title.
  PS3563.A2364S84 2013
  813'.54—dc23   2012046585

Published in 2013 by arrangement with Harlequin Books S.A.

Printed in Mexico
2 3 4 5 6 7 17 16 15 14 13

To the girls of Saint Joseph
Academy — Class of 1966

ONE

"You're going, aren't you?" Gloria Bailey asked for the third time.

And for the third time Jayne Gilbert stalled, taking a small bite of her egg-salad sandwich. She always ate egg salad on Tuesdays. "I don't know."

The invitation to her class reunion lay in the bottom of Jayne's purse, taunting her with memories she'd just as soon forget. The day was much too glorious to think about anything unpleasant. It was now mid-May, and the weather was finally warm enough to sit outside as they had lunch at a small café near the downtown Portland library.

"You'll regret it if you don't go," Gloria continued with a knowing look.

"You don't understand," Jayne said, pushing her glasses onto the bridge of her nose. She set aside the whole-wheat sandwich. "I was probably the only girl to graduate from St. Mary's in a state of grace."

Gloria tried unsuccessfully to swallow a chuckle.

"My whole senior year I had to listen while my classmates told marvelous stories about their backseat adventures," she said wryly. "I never had any adventures like that."

"And ten years later you still have no tales to tell?"

She nodded. "What's worse, all

those years have slipped by, and I've turned out exactly as my classmates predicted. I'm a librarian and living alone — *alone* being the operative word."

Jayne even looked the same. The frames of her glasses were more fashionable now, but her hair was the same shade of brown — the color of cedar chips, just a tad too dark to be termed mousy. She'd kept it the same length, too, although she preferred it clasped at the base of her neck these days. She no longer wore the school's uniform of red blazer jacket and navy pleated skirt, but she wore another one, of sorts. The straight black skirt or tailored pants, white silk blouse and business jacket were her daily attire.

Her romantic dreams had remained

dreams, and the love in her heart was showered generously upon the children who visited her regularly in the library. Jayne was the head of the children's department, while Gloria was a reference librarian. Both of them enjoyed their jobs.

"That's easy to fix," Gloria returned with a confidence Jayne lacked. "Go to the reunion looking different. Go dressed to the teeth, and bring along a gorgeous male who'll make you the envy of every girl in your class."

"I can't be something I'm not." Jayne didn't bother to mention the man. If she hadn't found a suitable male in ten years, what made Gloria think she could come up with one in two months?

"For one night you can be anything you want."

"It's *not* that easy," Jayne felt obliged to argue.

Until yesterday, before she'd sorted through her mail, she'd been content with her matter-of-fact existence. She liked her apartment and was proud of her accomplishments, however minor. Her life was uncomplicated, and frankly, she liked it that way.

But the last thing Jayne wanted was to go back and prove to her classmates that they'd been right. The thought was too humiliating. When she was a teenager, they'd taunted her as the girl most likely to succeed — behind the pages of a book. All her life, Jayne had been teased about her love for reading. Books were everything to her. She was the only child of doting parents who'd given up the hope of ever having children.

Although her parents had been thrilled at her late arrival, Jayne often wondered if they'd actually known what to do with her. Both were English professors at a Seattle college and it seemed natural to introduce her to their beloved world of literature at an early age. So Jayne had spent her childhood reading the classics when other girls were watching TV, playing outside and going to birthday parties. It wasn't until she reached her teens that she realized how much of a misfit she'd become. Oh, she had friends, lots of friends . . . Unfortunately the majority of them lived between the covers of well-loved books.

"You need a man like the one across the street," Gloria said.

"What man?" Jayne squinted.

"The one in the raincoat."

"Him?" The tall man resembled the mystery guy who lived in her apartment building. Jayne thought of him that way because he seemed to work the oddest hours. Twice she'd seen him in the apartment parking lot making some kind of transaction with another man. At the time she'd wondered if he was a drug dealer. She'd immediately discounted the idea as the result of an overactive imagination.

"*Look* at him, Jayne. He's a perfect male specimen. He's got that lean hardness women adore, and he walks as if he owns the street. A lot of women would go for him."

Watching the man her friend had pointed out, Jayne was even more convinced he was her neighbor.

They'd met a few times in the elevator, but they'd just exchanged nods; they'd never spoken. He lived on the same floor, three apartments down from hers. Jayne had been living near him for months and never really noticed the blatantly masculine features Gloria was describing.

"His jaw has that chiseled quality that drives women wild," Gloria was saying.

"I suppose," Jayne concluded, losing interest. She forced her attention back to her lunch. There was something about that man she didn't trust.

"Well, you aren't going to find someone to take to your class reunion by sitting around your apartment," Gloria muttered.

"I haven't decided if I'm going yet." But deep down, Jayne wanted to attend. No doubt it was some deep-seated masochistic tendency she had yet to analyze.

"You should go. I think you'd be surprised to see how everyone's changed."

That was the problem; Jayne *hadn't* changed. She still loved her books, and her life was even more organized now than it had been when she was in high school. Ten years after her graduation, she'd still be the object of their ridicule. "I don't know what I'm going to do," she announced, hoping to put an end to the discussion.

Hours later, at her apartment, Jayne sat holding a cup of green tea while she fantasized walking into the class reunion with a tall, strikingly handsome man. He would gaze into her eyes and bathe her in the warm glow of his love. And the girls of St. Mary's would sigh with envy.

The problem was where to find such a man. Not any man, but that special one who'd turn women's heads and make their hearts pound wildly.

Stretching out her legs and crossing her bare feet at the ankle, Jayne released a steady breath and conjured up her image of the perfect male. She'd read so many romances in her life, from the great classics to contemporary titles, that the vision of the ideal man — nothing like the one Gloria found so fascinating — appeared instantly in her mind. He would be tall, with thick, curly black hair and eyes of piercing blue. A man with sensitivity, desires and goals. Someone who'd accept her as she was . . . who'd think she was a special person. She wanted a man who could look past her imperfections and discover the woman inside.

A troubled frown creased her brow. She knew that for too many years, she'd buried herself in books, living her life vicariously through the escapades of others. The time had come to abandon her sedentary life and form a plan of action. Gloria was right — she wasn't going to find a man like that while sitting in her apartment. Drastic needs demanded drastic measures.

Rising to her feet Jayne took off her glasses and pulled the clasp from her hair. The curls cascaded over her shoulder, and she shook her head, freeing them. Plowing her fingers through her hair, she vowed to change. Or at least to try. Yes, she felt content with her life, but she had to admit there was something — or rather *someone* — missing.

Not until Jayne had left her apartment and was inside the elevator did it occur to her that she hadn't the slightest idea of where to meet men. Mentally she eliminated the spots she knew they congregated — places like taverns, pool halls and sports arenas. Her hero wasn't any of those types. A singles bar? Did people even use that term anymore? She'd never gone to one, but it sounded like just the place for a woman on a man-finding mission. Gloria would approve.

Jayne walked out of her building and ten minutes later, she sat in the corner of a cocktail lounge several blocks away. It had the rather obscure name of Soft Sam's. An embarrassed flush heated her face as she wondered what had possessed her to enter this place. Each time an eligible-looking man sauntered her way, she slid farther down into her chair, until she was so low her eyes were practically level with the table. The men in this bar were not the ones of which dreams were made. Thank goodness the room was as dark as a theater, with candles flickering atop the small round tables. The pulsing music, surly bartender and raised voices made her uncomfortable. Repeatedly she berated herself for doing anything as naive as coming here. Her parents would be aghast if they knew their sweet little girl was sitting in what they'd probably call a den of iniquity.

Forcing herself to straighten, Jayne's fingers coiled around her icy drink, and the chill extended halfway up her arm. According to what everyone said, the internet and a bar were the best ways to meet men. She was wary of resorting to online dating services, but she might have to consider it. And as for the bars . . . What her friends hadn't told her was the *type* of man who frequented such places. A glance around her confirmed that this was not where she belonged. Still, her goal was important. When she returned to Seattle, she was going to hold her head up high. There would be an incredible man on her arm, and she'd be the envy of every girl in her high school class. But if she had to lower her standards to this level, she'd rather not go back at all.

Her shoulders sagged with defeat. She'd been a fool to listen to Gloria. In her enthusiasm, Jayne had gone about this all wrong. A bar wasn't the place to begin her search; she should've realized that. *Books* would tell her what she needed to know. They'd never failed her yet, and she was astonished now that she could've forgotten something so basic.

Jayne squinted as she studied the men lined up at the polished bar. Even without her glasses, she could see that there wasn't a single man she'd consider taking to her reunion. The various women all seemed over-dressed and desperate. The atmosphere in the bar was artificial, the surface gaiety forced and frenetic.

Coming here tonight had been a

mistake. She felt embarrassed about letting down her hair and hiding her glasses in her purse — acting like someone she wasn't. The best thing to do now was to stand up and walk out of this place before someone actually approached her. But if it had taken courage to walk in, Jayne discovered that it took nearly as much to leave.

Unexpectedly the door of the lounge opened, dispersing a shaft of late-afternoon sunlight into the dim interior. Jayne pursed her lips, determined to escape. Turning to look at the latest arrival, she couldn't help staring. The situation was going from bad to intolerable. This man, whose imposing height was framed by the doorway, was the very one Gloria had been so excited about this afternoon.

He quickly surveyed the room, and Jayne recognized him; he was definitely her neighbor. The few times they'd met in the elevator, Jayne had sensed his disapproval. She didn't know what she'd done to offend him, but he seemed singularly unimpressed by her, and Jayne had no idea why. On second thought, Jayne told herself, he'd probably never given her a moment's notice. In fact, he'd probably paid as much attention to her as she had to him — almost none.

His large physique intimidated her, and the sharp glance he gave her was just short of unfriendly. He was more intriguing than good-looking. Though she knew that some women, like Gloria, found him attractive, his blunt features were far too rugged to classify as handsome. His hair was black and thick, and he was well over six feet tall. He walked with a hint of aggression in every stride. Jayne doubted he'd back down from a confrontation. She didn't know anything about him — not even his name — but she would've thought this was the last place he'd look for a date. But then, anyone who glanced at her would assume she didn't belong here, either. And she didn't.

Standing up, Jayne squared her shoulders and pushed back her chair while she studied the pattern on the carpet. Without raising her eyes, she fastened her raincoat and tucked her purse strap over her shoulder. The sooner she got out of this regrettable place, the better. She'd prefer to make her escape without attracting his attention, although with her hair down and without her glasses, it was unlikely that he'd recognize her.

Unfortunately her action caught his eye and he paused just inside the bar, watching her. Jayne hated the superior glare that burned straight through her. Blazing color moved up her neck and into her pale cheeks, but she refused to give him the satisfaction of lowering her gaze.

Jayne walked decisively toward the exit, which he was partially blocking. Something danced briefly in his dark blue eyes and she swallowed nervously. Slowly he stepped aside, but not enough to allow her to pass. The hard set of his mouth drew her attention. Her determined eyes met his. Brows as richly dark as his ebony hair rose slightly, and she saw a glimmer of arrogant amusement on his face.

"Well, well. If it isn't Miss Prim and Proper."

Jayne knew her expression must be horrified — he *had* recognized her — but she gritted her teeth, unwilling to acknowledge him. "If you'll excuse me, please."

"Of course," he murmured. He grinned as he gave her the necessary room. Jayne felt like running, her heart pounding as if she already had.

Humiliated, she hurried past him and stopped outside to hold her hand over her heart. As fast as her fingers would cooperate, she took her glasses from her purse. What on earth would he think of her being in a place like this? She didn't look like her normal self, but that hadn't fooled this sharp-eyed man. If he said something to her when they met again, she'd have an excuse planned.

She brushed the hair from her face and trekked down the sidewalk. He wouldn't say anything, she told herself. To imagine he'd even give her a second's thought would be overreacting. The only words he'd ever said to her had been that one taunting remark in the bar. It was unlikely that he'd strike up a conversation with her now. Especially since he so obviously found her laughable . . .

The following day at lunch, Jayne ordered Wednesday's roast-beef sandwich while Gloria chatted happily. "I've got the books on my desk."

"I only hope no one saw you take them."

"Not a soul," her friend said. "They look promising, particularly the one called *Eight Easy Steps to Meeting a Man.*"

"If you want, I'll pass it to you when I'm finished," Jayne offered.

"I just might take you up on that," Gloria surprised her by saying. Divorced for several years, she dated even less than Jayne did. "Don't act so shocked. I've been feeling the maternal urge lately. It would be nice to find a man and start a family."

The roast beef felt like a lead weight in the pit of Jayne's stomach. "Yes, it would," she agreed with a sigh. The worst thing about the lack of a husband was not having children. She always enjoyed them, and as the children's librarian she spent her days with other people's kids.

"I take it you've reconsidered my idea," Gloria continued.

"It might be worth a try." Jayne was much too embarrassed by her misadventure at the bar to say anything to her friend about it.

"You know, if that *was* your neighbor yesterday, you don't need to look too hard."

As far as Jayne was concerned, she never wanted to see *him* again.

"I suppose," she mumbled. "But I'd like to find a man with more . . . culture."

"Up to you," Gloria said, shaking her head.

The same afternoon, her arms loaded with borrowed books on meeting men, Jayne stepped onto the elevator — and came face-to-face with her neighbor. Her first instinct was to turn around and dash out again. His eyes darkened with challenge as they met hers, and she refused to give him the satisfaction of letting him know how much he unnerved her. With all the dignity she could muster, Jayne moved to the rear of the elevator, feeling unreasonably angry with Gloria.

His eyes flickered over her flushed face. Reaction more than need prompted her to push up her glasses, and she struggled to disguise her nervousness with deep breaths.

"Ninth floor, right?" he murmured.

"Yes." Her voice came out sounding like a frog with laryngitis. She'd been so flustered she hadn't even punched in her floor number. Hugging the books to her chest, she kept her eyes on the orange light that indicated the numbers above the elevator door.

"I have to admit it was a surprise seeing you last night," he said smoothly, clearly enjoying her discomfort.

Hot color flashed from her face like a neon light. "I beg your pardon?" If she could have gotten away with it, she would have given him a frown of utter bewilderment, as if to say she had no idea what he was talking about. But Jayne had never been a good liar. Her eye would twitch and her upper lip quiver. Fooling her parents had been impossible; she wouldn't dream of trying to deceive this way-too-perceptive man.

"I didn't know prim and proper little girls went into bars like that."

Clearing her throat, she sent him a look of practiced disdain usually reserved for teenagers she caught necking in the upstairs portion of the library. "Let me assure you, I am not the type of woman who frequents such places." She wished she didn't sound quite so stilted, and for the twentieth time in as many hours, she lamented her foolishness. Her back and shoulders ached with the effort to stand there rigidly. If he knew anything about body language, he'd get her message.

"You're telling me," he said and chuckled softly. Mischief glimmered in his eyes, and with an effort Jayne looked away.

"You must have mistaken me for someone else," she told him sternly, disgusted with herself for lying. Immediately her right eye started to twitch, and her grip on the books tightened. The elevator had never made its ascent more slowly. She finally relaxed when it came to a grinding halt on her floor. The minute the door opened she rushed out. In her haste, her shoe snagged on the thick carpet and propelled her forward. With a cry of alarm she went staggering into the wide hallway, the books flying from her arms. The wall opposite the elevator halted her progress when she was catapulted into it, catching herself with open palms.

"Are you okay?" A gentle hand touched her shoulder. She turned and gave a convulsive jerk of her head as humiliation robbed her of speech. The dark eyes that had been probing hers were now filled with concern.

"I — I'm fine," she managed, wiping a shaking hand over her eyes, hoping to wake and find that this entire episode was a nightmare.

"Let me help you with your books."

"No!" she cried breathlessly and scrambled to gather up her collection. The last thing she wanted was his pity. He'd made his feelings known. He didn't think much of her, but he was entitled to his opinion — and his fun. "I'm fine. Just leave. Please. That's all I want." She was only getting what she deserved for behaving so irrationally and going into that stupid bar in the first place. Now she'd made everything worse. Never had she felt more embarrassed, and it was all her own fault.

Her hands shook as she fumbled with the clasp of her purse and took out her apartment key. She didn't turn around, but she could feel his eyes on her. Her whole body was trembling by the time she entered the apartment. She shut the door and leaned against it, closing her eyes.

Several minutes passed before she was able to remove her coat and pile the books on her kitchen table. She hung her coat in the hall closet, went into her bedroom and set her purse on the dresser. Organization gave guidance and balance to Jayne's life, and there was never a time she'd needed it more.

The teapot was filled and heating on the stove. Trying to put the unfortunate encounter in the elevator out of her mind, she looked through the books she'd brought home. *Finding a Man in Thirty Days or Less* was the first book in the stack. That one sounded helpful. She glanced at the next one, *How to Get a Man Interested in You*. These self-help books would provide all the advice she needed, Jayne mused. And if they worked for her, she'd pass them on to Gloria later. As always, Jayne would find the answer in books. The next title made her smile. *How to Convince a Man to Fall in Love with You Forever*. Nice thought, but all she really cared about right now was the one night of her class reunion.

She heard knocking and lifted her head abruptly, then slowly moved to the door, her legs weighted by reluctance. She was acquainted with only a few people in Portland. There was no one, other than Gloria, whom she'd call a good friend.

"Who is it?" she asked.

"Riley Chambers."

"Who?"

"Your neighbor."

Groaning inwardly, Jayne closed her eyes, dreading the thought of seeing him again for any reason. Hesitantly she turned the lock. "I'm perfectly fine," she said, opening the door.

"I thought you might be looking for this." He leaned against the doorjamb, leafing indolently through the pages of a hardcover book.

Jayne's breath jammed in her throat as she struggled not to grab it from his hands. Noting the title, *How to Pick Up a Man,* she felt her face redden.

Brilliant little flecks of light showed in his eyes, which glinted with humor. "Listen, Ms. Gilbert, if you're so interested in finding yourself a man, I'd advise you to stay away from bars like Soft Sam's. They're not good places for little girls like you."

She frowned. "How do you know my name? Oh — the building directory."

He nodded.

"Well, *Mr. Chambers,* if you've come to make fun of me . . ."

"I haven't." The expression in his eyes hardened. "I don't want to ever see you there again."

"You have no business telling me where I can and cannot go." Her hands knotted at her sides in outrage. He was right, of course, but she had no intention of letting him know that. She jerked the book from his hand and when he stepped away, she slammed the door.

Two

Riley dropped his arms and grinned at the door that had closed in his face. So prim little Ms. Gilbert had a fiery temper. She might act like a shy country mouse, but his opinion of her went up several notches. With that well-tamed hair and those glasses, she hadn't left much of an impression the few times he'd seen her in the elevator. Her air of blind trust and hopeful expectation made her look as though she'd stepped out of the pages of a Victorian novel. She'd better watch out, or she'd be wolves' prey. He'd wanted to tell her to open her eyes and look around her. She was too vulnerable for this day and age. This was the twenty-first century, not some romantic daydream.

It'd surprised him to see her in Soft Sam's. Admittedly, she'd been a fish out of water. She was absolutely correct; it was none of his business where she went, but he felt oddly protective of her.

Ms. J. Gilbert — he didn't even know her first name — was as untouched and naive as they come. All sugar and spice and everything nice. Rubbing a hand over the back of his neck, Riley sighed impatiently. He didn't have time to think about a woman — any woman. But a smile formed as he recalled the fire that had flared in her eyes when she'd grabbed that book from his hands. She had spunk. Briefly he wondered what other treasures were waiting to be discovered in her. Riley gave himself a mental shake. Years of following his instincts told him that women like this could be trouble for men like him. Besides, his days were filled with enough conflict. He didn't need a woman distracting him from the problems at hand. Maybe when this business with Priestly was over, he'd have the time — No! The best thing he could do was forget Ms. Sugar and Spice.

If she was in the market for a husband — which she obviously was — there were better men. She was far too wide-eyed and innocent for him. In the end he'd only hurt her. She

deserved someone who hadn't become cynical, who wasn't hardened
by life.

Jayne stared out at the rain that rolled
down the side of the grimy bus window. A low gray fog hovered over the
street. After five years in Portland,
she was accustomed to gloomy
springs. The paper lay folded in her
lap; the headlines were the same day
after day, although the names and
places changed. War, death, disease
and destruction. She saw that a
prominent state official had been
questioned by the FBI about ties to
the underworld. Jayne wondered if
Senator Priestly was one of the of-
ficials who'd visited the library recently. She'd been impressed with the
group on the tour; there had been a

number of men Gloria would have approved of. But then, that could mean neither Gloria nor Jayne was a good judge of character.

Riley Chambers was a perfect example of their poor judgment. He might not have been impressed with her, but from the first she'd thought he was . . . intriguing. A man of mystery. Despite the fact that they'd barely glanced at each other whenever they'd met in the elevator, she *might* have been interested in getting to know him. Her current opinion was decidedly different. He had a lot of nerve telling her not to go back to Soft Sam's! If it was such a terrible place, what was he doing there? The next time she saw him, she'd make a point of asking him exactly that.

Agitated, she pulled the cord to

indicate that she wanted to get off at the next stop. She tucked the newspaper under her arm and hurried to the rear of the bus.

Avoiding a puddle, she leapt from the bottom step to the sidewalk and paused to open her umbrella. Riley Chambers didn't deserve another minute of her consideration. He'd made his views of her obvious. He'd called her a little girl. She had a good mind to inform him that at five-seven she could hardly be described as *little*. Even now his taunting comment rankled. Jayne had the feeling that he'd said it just to get a reaction out of her. Well, he'd succeeded, and that should please him.

Gloria was waiting for her when Jayne arrived at the library.

"Well, what did the books say?" her

friend asked as soon as Jayne had put her bag inside her desk.

"Plenty. Did you know one of the best places to meet men is in the supermarket? Can you see me sauntering up to someone in the frozen-food section and suggesting we have children together?"

Gloria's laughter floated around the room. "That may be worth a try. What other place did they suggest?"

"The art gallery."

"That's perfect for you!"

Jayne sighed and tucked a stray curl into her tightly coiled chignon. "I suppose."

"You've got to show more enthusiasm than this, m'dear." Opening the paper on Jayne's desk, Gloria ran down a list of current city events.

"The Portland Art Gallery is show-

ing work by one of your favorite art-
ists — Delacroix. I bet you were planning on attending, anyway. Now all
you need to do is keep your eyes
peeled for any handsome, eligible
men."

"I don't know, Gloria. I can't even
catch a cold, let alone a man. Especially a handsome one."

"You can do it."

"Now you sound like a cheer-
leader," Jayne moaned, not sure she
wanted any of this.

"You need me," Gloria insisted.
"Look upon me as your own personal
cheering section. All I ask is that you
think of God, country and your best
friend as you stroll through that gallery."

"What?"

"Well, if this works for you, then I

may give it a try."

Jayne had her doubts. Over the past several years, she'd visited a variety of galleries and had yet to see a single attractive man. However, she hadn't actually been on the lookout.

"Well?" Gloria stared at her with her hands positioned challengingly on her hips. "Are you or are you not going to the Delacroix show?"

"Gloria . . ." Jayne said, hedging.

"Jayne!"

"Fine, I'll go."

"When?"

"Tomorrow afternoon."

Although she might have agreed to Gloria's suggestion, Jayne wasn't sure she was doing the right thing. All day she fretted about the coming art show. By five she was a nervous wreck. Feeling that she needed the confidence a new outfit would give her, Jayne decided to go shopping after work. This was no easy decision. She equated clothes-shopping with trauma. Nothing ever seemed to fit well, and she dreaded standing in front of those three-way mirrors that revealed every imperfection.

At the end of the day, Jayne walked down the library steps, balking at the thought of this expedition. Sheer force of will led her into The Galleria, the downtown shopping center, where she found a navy wool dress with side pockets and long sleeves. The dress didn't do much for her, but it was the first one that fit without looking like a burlap bag flung over her head. Feeling somewhat relieved, she paid the saleslady and headed for the escalator that would take her to the transit mall. On her way out Jayne noticed a young woman draped on the arm of a much older man. She batted her long lashes and paused at an expensive jeweler's window display.

"Last month's emerald is so, so lonely," Jayne heard the woman's soft voice purr.

"We can't have that, can we, darling," the older man murmured as he steered the blonde inside the store.

The episode left a bad taste in Jayne's mouth, and she wondered if the woman had met her sugar daddy in Safeway. It was beyond her imagination that men would be attracted to women so shallow. If this was the type of behavior men sought, Jayne simply couldn't do it.

■ ■ ■ ■

Saturday afternoon, wearing her new dress, Jayne strolled bravely through the Portland Art Gallery. Wandering around, she saw a man standing against a wall; he seemed to be more interested in the patrons than the art. Gathering her nerve and her resolve, she stood in front of a Delacroix painting, *Horse Frightened by a Storm,* the most famous of the paintings on loan from the Seattle Art Museum. Jayne had long been an admirer of Delacroix's work and knew it well. He was, in her opinion, the greatest of the Romantic painters.

Again she studied the man, sizing him up without, she hoped, being too obvious. He was attractive, although it was difficult to tell for sure without her glasses. From what she could see, he looked approachable. Her hands felt clammy, and she resisted the urge to wipe them dry on the sides of her dress. Clearly she didn't know much about luring a man. But neither was she totally ignorant. She *had* dated before and had even felt the faint stirrings of desire. But her relationships usually died a natural death from lack of nourishment. Sad as it seemed, Jayne preferred her books.

She moved across the marble floor toward the man. Coming closer, she confirmed that he was attractive in a slender, refined way — not like Riley Chambers. Just the thought of *that* arrogant man brought a flash of hot color to her cheeks.

Trying to ignore the tension that

knotted her stomach, Jayne mentally reviewed the books she'd read. Each had repeatedly stated that she couldn't wait for the man to take the initiative. One book had gone so far as to list ways of starting a conversation with a prospective love interest. Fumbling her purse clasp, Jayne pulled out the list of ideas she'd jotted down. She could ask for change for the parking meter, but she didn't own a car and lying would make her eye twitch. She discarded that plan. Next on the list was pretending not to notice the targeted male and accidentally-on-purpose walking straight into him. Too clichéd, Jayne decided. She wanted to be more original. The book had suggested asking him what time it was. Okay, she could try that.

Dropping the list in her purse, she took three strides toward the blonde man and did an abrupt about-face. She was wearing a watch! How could she ask the time when there was a watch on her wrist? She'd look like an idiot!

Jayne's heart felt as though it was pounding right out of her chest. Who would've supposed that anything this simple could be so difficult? Sighing, she remembered the look Gloria had given her as she hustled her out the door of the library. If she didn't make her move, Gloria would never let her live it down.

Eyes closed, she took slow, even breaths until calm reason returned. This whole idea was ludicrous. Dressing up and loitering around an art gallery hoping to meet men was so contrary to her painfully shy personality that she could hardly believe she was doing it. The girls of St. Mary's wouldn't be impressed by such desperate measures. Who did Jayne think she was going to fool? She'd turned out exactly as they'd predicted, and there was nothing she could do to change that.

"Excuse me." A male voice interrupted her thoughts. "Do you happen to have the time?"

Jayne's eyes flew open. "The time," she repeated.

The man Jayne had noticed came to stand beside her. Instantly her eyes went to her wrist. He must have read the same book!

"I'm afraid I forgot to replace the battery in my watch," he said with a sheepish smile, dispelling that notion.

"It's nearly three," she stammered, holding out her arm so he could examine her watch.

"I saw you were looking at the Delacroix painting of the horse."

"Yes," Jayne murmured. It'd worked! It had really worked. She smiled up at him brightly, remembering the adoring look on the young woman's face as she'd stared into the eyes of her sugar daddy.

"By the way, my name's Mark Bauer."

"Jayne Gilbert," she said and offered him her hand. Recalling "darling's" reactions, Jayne lowered her lashes alluringly so that they brushed the arch of her cheek.

"He's my favorite artist — Eugene Delacroix." Mark gestured at the painting with one hand.

Ferdinand Victor Eugene Delacroix, Jayne added mentally.

"When Delacroix died in 1863 he left behind a legacy of eight hundred oil paintings," Mark lectured.

And twice as many watercolors, Jayne said — but only to herself. "Is that a fact?" she simpered.

Warming to his subject, Mark continued by explaining the familiar painting, pointing out the colors chosen by the artist to establish mood. He went on to describe how particular lines in the work expressed certain feelings. Jayne batted her lashes at Mark and pretended to be impressed by his knowledge. She wished she had her glasses on so she could see more clearly what he looked like. From a distance he'd appeared attractive enough; close up he was a little blurry.

By the time Jayne was on the bus for the return trip to her apartment, she was thoroughly disgusted with herself. She wasn't any better than that syrupy blonde clinging to the arm of her generous benefactor. She was sure she knew much more about art than Mark did and yet she'd played dumb. He'd apparently done a quick search on Google to collect some basic facts, then spun them into the art history lecture she'd just heard. And she'd pretended to be awed. . . .

Something was definitely wrong with her. She'd always been such a sensible woman. It astonished her that Mark hadn't seen through her act. She wasn't convinced she even liked the man. He spoke for half an hour on a subject he obviously knew very little about while Jayne continued to play dumb and batted her lashes every ten seconds. She supposed he was hoping to impress her, but, in fact, had accomplished just the opposite. The whole production had been pointless — for both of them. He'd asked for her phone number, but she figured she'd never hear from him again.

A walk in the park helped her clear away the confusion that clouded her perspective. She'd thought she'd known what she wanted. Suddenly she was unsure. Knights riding around on white horses, looking for women to escort to class reunions, seemed to be few and far between these days. But then, she didn't know much about knights and even less about men. Quite possibly, each and every one of them would turn out to be like Riley Chambers. The thought caused a shiver of apprehension to race over her skin and she realized for the first time that a slow drizzling rain had begun to fall. Of course, she'd left her umbrella at home. And of course there were no cabs in sight.

Burying her hands deep in her pockets, she quickened her pace. She was three blocks from her building when the clouds burst open in sheets of rain that pelted the sidewalk relentlessly. Jayne was drenched within seconds. Rivulets of water ran down the back of her neck until her hair fell in limp strands. When she stepped into the lobby, her glasses fogged, and her new dress was plastered to her. She felt the overwhelming desire to sneeze. This had been the most miserable day of her life. Not only had she behaved like an idiot over the first man to fall in with her schemes, but she'd been foolish enough to get caught in a downpour. The only thing worse would be to run into Riley Chambers.

No sooner had the thought formed than the man materialized.

Jayne groaned inwardly and stepped into the open elevator, praying he'd take another. The way her luck was going, Jayne should have known better.

Riley followed her inside and stared blatantly at the half-drowned country mouse, a small puddle of water form- ing at her feet. He couldn't resist a tiny smile as he studied her. Ms. J.

Gilbert was badly in need of someone to watch over her. He hadn't seen her in the past couple of days, and it hadn't taken long to realize she was avoiding him. That was fine. She brought out his protective instincts with those wide, innocent eyes, which was something he couldn't really afford. She disturbed him, and innumerable times in the past two days thoughts of her had flitted through his head. Casually he'd tossed them aside, chalking up his curiosity to concern that she might go back to Soft Sam's.

Jayne turned her head away. "Go ahead and laugh," she told him as they began their slow ascent. "I know you're dying to make fun of me."

Riley scowled briefly. Suddenly she reminded him of a cat backed into a corner, its fur bristling and claws unsheathed. Riley had no desire to antagonize her. Instead, he felt the urge to comfort her — and that astonished him. "Are you still angry because I saw the title of your book?" he asked.

"Furious." She slipped her steamed glasses to the end of her nose so she could see him above the frames.

"I didn't mean to make fun of you." She looked vulnerable, and he ignored the impulse to ask her first name. He didn't see her as a Jessica or a Jennifer. Possibly a Jacqueline.

"Why not make fun of me?" she flared. "Everyone else has . . . all my life. People have always thought I'm some kind of weirdo. I like books. I like to read." He saw tears in her eyes, and she twisted around so he couldn't look at her.

The instant the elevator doors parted, she escaped, her shoulders back, her head held high, and glided down the hall to her apartment.

Riley went to his own door, walking slowly. He withdrew the keys from his pocket with a frown, then wearily turned the lock and stepped into his dark apartment. A flick of the wall switch flooded the room with cheerless light. He threw his raincoat over the back of a chair and went into the kitchen to put a frozen dinner in the microwave.

Once again the little mouse, as he still thought of her, had fired to life, turning on him. Even cold and miserable, she'd walked out of the elevator with her chin raised. Her back was ramrod straight, and she moved with as much dignity as any princess. He smiled as he recalled the way her wet dress had clung to her, revealing full breasts, round hips and a trim waist. She had long legs, nicely shaped. He couldn't imagine why she chose to hide behind those generic business suits. The dress she wore today was the first he could remember seeing her in. The dark navy color wasn't right for her. With that chestnut hair and those large honey-brown eyes she should wear lighter shades. At least she'd had her hair down, which was a definite improvement. Although it had been wet and clinging, he just knew it was soft. Silky. He wanted to lift it in his fingers and —

Slumping into a chair, Riley shook his head. He didn't like the things Ms. J. Gilbert brought to the surface in him. It had been a lot of years since he'd given a woman this much thought. What he felt was pity, he assured himself. She was lonely. For that matter, so was he.

The microwave made its annoying sound, and he removed the tray, wondering what the country mouse was having for her dinner.

Holding a tissue to her nose, Jayne sneezed loudly. Her eyes itched, and her throat felt scratchy. A glance at her watch told her it would be another three long hours before she could go home and soak in a hot tub. Thankfully Gloria had offered to handle story-time today. While the preschoolers huddled around her friend, Jayne sat at her desk and cut out brightly colored letters for the

June bulletin board. Her class reunion was only seven weeks away. Like the ominous approach of a thunderstorm, defeat settled over her. She wouldn't go. It was as simple as that.

"Could you tell me where you keep the biographies?"

She raised her eyes, and they met a familiar blue gaze. Riley Chambers . . . She clutched the scissors so hard that her thumb ached. "Pardon?" Stunned, she couldn't remember what he'd asked.

"The biographies."

In an effort to stall for time, she put the scissors down. Riley Chambers was on her turf now. "They're directly to your left."

"Could you show me where they are?"

"Yes, of course, but you look like a man who knows his way around."

"Not in this library," he mumbled.

She stood, pausing to push the glasses up onto her nose, then led him to the section he'd requested. "The area to the right is the children's fiction department for ages three to six. If you like, we'll stop here so you can browse."

Riley ignored that. He'd had one heck of a time finding out where she worked. Their apartment manager had to have the most closed mouth of anyone he'd ever known. Generally speaking, he approved of that, but with a lie about undefined but urgent "legal matters," he'd managed to get his answer. "The name Jayne suits you," he said. He'd seen the nameplate on her desk.

"As long as you aren't Tarzan."

"I don't live in a jungle."

"But you obviously speak the language." A smile tugged at the corner of her mouth.

After delivering Riley to the section he'd requested, Jayne watched as he took down several volumes and flipped through the pages. She studied him with helpless fascination. Riley Chambers was a cynical man who looked at the world through wary eyes. Nonetheless, she had a glimmer — more than a glimmer — of his sensuality. Horrified at her thoughts, Jayne quickly returned to her desk. She resumed her task, doing her best to pretend he wasn't anywhere around.

"I'd like to check these out," Riley said, setting two thick volumes on the corner of her desk.

"Do you have a library card?"

"Yeah. It's tricky borrowing books without one."

"You don't need me for that." Jayne didn't know why he'd come. He probably wanted to throw her off guard. That wasn't going to work. Not in the library.

"I assumed that as a public employee you'd be willing to help me."

"Books are checked out at the front desk."

"I want you to do it."

"Why?"

"Why not?"

"I'm the children's librarian."

"That doesn't surprise me. You look like someone who'd prefer the world of make-believe and happy ever after."

"Is that so wrong?" she replied, her temper flaring.

"Just as long as you don't expect to find your heroes in a sleazy bar."

Color heated Jayne's already flushed face, and she glanced around, wondering if Gloria had heard him. Gloria raised her head long enough to wink encouragingly. "Why are you here?" Jayne whispered.

"You confuse me," he admitted after a minute. "Or maybe *disturb* would be a better word."

"Why?"

"I don't know. Probably because you look like an accident waiting to happen."

"I don't need a fairy godfather." Not when Gloria insisted on waving a magic wand over her head every morning.

"I know what you're after," he whispered back. "I saw the book, remember?"

Jayne bit her lip. Riley was playing with her, amusing himself at her expense. "I'm not looking for a husband. I . . . only need a man for one night."

"So that's it." The corner of his mouth edged up.

"No!" she cried at his knowing look. Her cry attracted the attention of the entire room. The library went silent as heads turned toward them. Embarrassed half to death, Jayne lowered her chin and pleaded, "Would you please just go away?"

Riley abandoned his books and stalked outside, berating himself with every step. Talk about stupid! What kind of game did he think he was playing? Earlier that afternoon the workload had gotten to him, and when he couldn't tolerate it anymore, he'd leaned back in his chair and closed his eyes. A picture of the alluring Jayne Gilbert, all sugar and spice, had immediately entered his mind. He didn't know why she fascinated him so much. Maybe it was because of her innocence, her gentle beauty and the goodness he sensed in her.

After a day like this one, he needed some of that innocence. It'd taken him the better part of an hour to get the information about her job out of the building manager. Discovering she was a librarian hadn't come as any surprise. It fit his image of her. But showing up here hadn't been one of his more brilliant ideas. He hadn't meant to browbeat Jayne and he'd been amused by her witty comebacks. She'd held her own.

Feeling angry and frustrated with himself, Riley went back to the office. He'd apologize to her later. Ms. Gilbert deserved that much.

By the time all the paperwork had been cleared from his desk, it was close to eight. He rubbed a hand over his face, feeling more tired than he'd been in years. He was getting too old for this work. Grabbing his jacket from the back of his chair, Riley tossed his empty paper cup into the garbage can. He hadn't had anything but coffee since early afternoon. The way things were going in this madhouse, it was a miracle he didn't have an ulcer.

Once he'd parked in the apartment

lot and headed across the street to the building, thoughts of Jayne flooded his mind. He sighed, unable to disperse them.

The elevator stopped on the ninth floor. He stood for a full minute outside her door before deciding it would be better to get this apology over with. He knocked once, loudly.

Jayne was miserable. Her throat felt like fire every time she swallowed. Her head ached, and the last thing she wanted was company. Housecoat cinched tight around her waist, she unlocked the door.

"You again?" she whispered, hardly caring. "What's the matter, didn't you have enough fun earlier?"

Riley disregarded her comment. "You look awful."

"Thanks."

"Are you sick?"

"No," she answered hoarsely and coughed. "I enjoy looking like this."

Without an invitation, Riley walked into her apartment and demanded, "Have you seen a doctor?"

Jayne stood by the door, holding it open and staring pointedly into the empty hallway. "Make yourself at home," she said with heavy sarcasm. As it was, she'd spent a good part of the afternoon explaining Riley's visit to Gloria. Somehow her friend refused to believe it was a coincidence that he'd come into the library. According to Gloria, Riley was definitely interested in Jayne. That suggestion only made her laugh.

"You might have a fever. Have you taken your temperature?"

"I was about to do that." The man appeared oblivious to her lack of welcome. She closed the door and turned around, leaning against it.

"Sit down," he said.

"Are you always this bossy?"

"Always."

Too weak to argue, Jayne did as he said.

"Where's your thermometer?"

She pointed to the kitchen counter and tucked her bare feet underneath her. "Why do you keep pestering me?"

He didn't respond, seemingly intent on reading the thermometer. Impatiently he shook it.

"Open your mouth," he ordered, and when she complied, he gently inserted it under her tongue.

Curious, Jayne followed his progress

as he paced the carpet in front of her, checking his watch every fifteen seconds. He picked up a book from the coffee table, read the title and arched his brows. Replacing the book, he resumed his pacing.

"I came because I wanted to apologize for this afternoon. I had no business, uh, pestering you."

"Then why did you?" she mumbled, holding the thermometer in her mouth as she spoke.

"I don't know." His hand sliced the air. "Probably for the reason I mentioned earlier. You . . . disturb me."

"Why?" she asked again.

"If I knew the answer to that, I wouldn't be here."

"Then go away."

"I thought misery loved company."

"Not this misery."

"Too bad." Carefully he withdrew the thermometer and examined it.

"Well? What does it say? Will I live?"

"A little over ninety-nine. Got any aspirin?"

Jayne shook her head. "I'm never sick."

He studied her skeptically, and Jayne waited for a harangue that never came.

"I'll be back." He left her door slightly ajar, and Jayne felt too miserable to get up and lock him out.

Riley returned a couple of minutes later, his arms loaded with a variety of objects: soup can, a box of tissues, bottle of aspirin, frozen lemonade and the paper.

"Are you moving in?" she asked irritably. The other day she'd assumed that she couldn't meet a man in her own living room. Riley was proving her wrong.

He scowled and stalked wordlessly into her tiny kitchen. What an odd man he was, Jayne thought. He obviously felt *something* for her if he was going to all this trouble, and yet he didn't seem to want her company.

After a moment Jayne decided to investigate. Struggling to her feet, she paused in the middle of the room to sneeze and blow her nose.

Riley stuck his head around the corner. "Sit," he ordered, giving her a ferocious glare.

Jayne glared back at him. "What are you doing in my kitchen?"

"Making dinner. Don't be ungrateful."

"I'm not hungry," she said, advancing a step. Riley would never be able to figure out her organizational methods. He'd look in her cupboards and claim that even her groceries were filed under the Dewey decimal system.

"Is it feed a cold and starve a fever or the other way around?" Riley asked next.

He made quite a sight with his white shirtsleeves rolled halfway up his arms and an apron tied high around his waist. The top two buttons of his shirt were opened to reveal dark curling hair. Jayne couldn't help smiling.

"Now what's so funny?" His own smile was lazy.

"You."

"What?" He glanced down at his flowered apron. "What's the matter, haven't you ever seen a man working in the kitchen?"

"Not in mine."

"Then it's time you did." He turned away from her and took a saucepan from the top of the stove, then opened and closed her cupboard doors until he located glasses and bowls. "You should smile more often," he said casually as he worked, pouring equal amounts of soup into the wide bowls.

"I've got a cold. My head hurts, my throat feels raw, and there's a crazy man in my kitchen, ordering me around. Give me a day or two, and I'll find the humor in all of this." She didn't add that she had seven weeks to come up with a man who'd make heads turn when he walked into a room.

"Sit."

"Again? See what I mean?" she complained, but she did as he asked, pulling out the high-backed oak chair.

Riley brought her a bowl of hot soup, a steaming mug and two aspirin. Jerking the apron from around his waist, he took the chair across from her.

"What is it?" she asked, staring at the steaming bowl.

"Chicken noodle soup." He pointed to the bowl, then the mug. "And hot lemonade."

"Couldn't you be more original than that?"

"Not on short notice."

"Are you eating here, too?"

"What's the matter? Do you expect the help to eat in the kitchen?"

Jayne smiled again. "Why are you

doing this?"

Riley shrugged. "Because I owe you. I didn't mean to make fun of you earlier."

"When?" To her way of thinking, he'd done it more than once.

"This afternoon. I shouldn't have come in and given you a hard time. I want to apologize."

"If you're in the mood to make amends, you might mention the other night, as well."

"No." He scowled briefly, letting his eyes drop to her lips. "You brought that on yourself."

Jayne set her spoon aside. "I don't know if I like you. I've never met anyone who confuses me the way you do."

"Then that makes two of us. Listen, I've lived most of my life without women, and I don't want a prim little country mouse messing things up at this late date." The words were harsher than he'd intended, but Jayne was stronger than her soft, vulnerable manner had led him to believe. She had an inner strength he was only beginning to recognize.

Jayne bristled, her hand gripping the spoon tightly. "I didn't invite you here." She'd have a heck of a time explaining this to Gloria if her friend ever found out.

"I'm aware of that."

The phone rang, jerking Jayne's attention across the room.

"Do you want me to answer it?" Riley asked.

"No," she answered, rising from her chair. "I will." She reached the phone on the fourth ring and grabbed it.

"Hello," she said, slightly out of breath.

"Jayne, it's Mark Bauer. Do you remember me? We met at the art gallery last Saturday."

THREE

"Hello, Mark, of course I remember you." Jayne leaned against the chair, trying to ignore Riley, who was standing behind her.

"You don't sound the same," Mark continued.

"I've got a cold." That had to be the understatement of the year.

"Not a bad one, I hope."

"Oh, no, I'll be fine in a day or two." Muffled sounds coming from behind Jayne made her tense. Riley was either pacing or fooling around in her kitchen. She wondered if he'd discovered how organized she was. Even her soup cans were stored in alphabetical order.

"Do you think you'd be well enough to go to a movie with me Friday night?" Mark asked.

Jayne was stunned. After behaving in such a ridiculous way, she hadn't expected to hear from Mark again. Least of all to have him ask her out. "I'd like that, thank you."

"Shall we say seven, then?"

"Seven will be fine."

Jayne replaced the receiver and stared at the phone, dumbfounded. A prickly feeling attacked the base of her neck and slithered down her spine. The dumb act had worked once, but she doubted she could maintain it for any length of time. Keeping it up for the seven weeks until her class reunion would be impossible. And once they were in Seattle, she couldn't suddenly tell him: *Surprise! It was all an act. I'm really brilliant.* "I shouldn't have agreed to go." Jayne was shocked to realize she'd spoken aloud.

"Why not?"

Feeling a bit sick to her stomach, Jayne turned to face Riley, who was standing beside the kitchen table. One large hand rested over the back of the polished oak chair. Their eyes met. "I . . . don't know exactly what he looks like," she admitted honestly, but that wasn't the reason for her hesitancy. Someone like Riley would have instantly seen through her act. Unfortunately — or fortunately — Mark wasn't Riley.

"What do you mean?"

"When we met, I wasn't wearing my glasses." Jayne vowed that if Riley so much as snickered, she'd ask him to leave.

"If wearing glasses bothers you, why don't you get contacts?" he asked matter-of-factly, reaching for his spoon. That night at Soft Sam's she hadn't worn her glasses, he remembered and stiffened.

"I've tried but I can't. My eye doctor recommended a book on how to use them, but . . ."

"It didn't help you?"

Jayne lowered her hands to her lap. "Sadly, no."

"Where did you meet this Mark guy?" He struggled to keep his voice calm and disinterested. He'd been trained not to reveal interest or emotion. It should come easy, but with

Jayne, for some reason, it didn't.

"At the art gallery last Saturday." She caught a sneeze with her napkin just in time. "One of those books said that was a good place to meet men."

Relaxing, Riley tried his first spoonful of lukewarm chicken noodle soup. He might not be an inventive chef, but this meager meal would take the edge off his hunger. The fact that Jayne was sitting across from him with her quiet wit and seductive eyes made even soup more appealing.

They ate in silence, but it was a companionable one as if they were at ease with each other for the first time. Jayne wasn't hungry, but she managed to finish her soup. Riley insisted on doing the dishes, and she didn't argue too strenuously. There were only a couple of bowls and a saucepan that he rinsed and tucked in the dishwasher.

"Is there anything else I can do for you?" Riley asked, standing by the door.

Jayne smiled shyly and shook her head. "No, you've been very kind. Thank you." He was an attractive man, and she didn't know why he was paying her so much attention. His concern was so unexpected that she didn't know how to categorize it. They were neighbors, and it would be good to have a friend in the apartment complex. Riley was probably thinking the same thing, Jayne mused. Their relationship was mutually beneficial.

"I'll see you later," he said.

"Later," she agreed.

■ ■ ■ ■

The next morning, Jayne woke feeling a hundred percent better. The ache in her throat was gone, as was the stiffness in her arms and legs. Declaring herself cured, she dressed for work, humming as she moved around the bedroom. For several days she'd been dreading the approach of summer and her class reunion, but this morning things looked brighter. Mark had asked her out, and she was determined to keep his interest in her alive. That shouldn't be difficult with Gloria's coaching.

Although the day was predicted to be pleasantly warm, Jayne reached for her jacket on the way out the door. She half looked for Riley as she waited for the elevator, but she'd only seen him a few times in the mornings. Their paths didn't cross often. She would like to have told him how much better she felt and thank him again for his help.

Standing at the bus stop, she noticed that the clouds were breaking up. The air smelled fresh and springlike. Jayne had to remember that this was June, yet it felt more like April or early May. School would be out soon, and her section of the library would be busier than usual.

When a sleek black car pulled up by the curb, Jayne instinctively stepped back, then experienced a flush of pleasure when she recognized the driver.

Riley leaned across the front seat and opened the side door. "It might not be a good idea for you to stand out in the cold. I'll give you a ride downtown."

"I feel great this morning," she told him. "Thanks for the offer," she felt obliged to say, "but the bus will be here any minute."

Riley's grip tightened on the door handle. "I'll give you a ride if you want. The choice is yours." He said it without looking at her.

Jayne still didn't understand why he was so concerned about her health, but now wasn't the time to question his solicitude. She slid into the front seat, closed the door and fastened her seat belt. "You're going to spoil me, Mr. Chambers."

"I don't work far from you," he said, checking the side mirror before merging with the snarled traffic.

That explained why she and Gloria had seen him at lunchtime. Jayne studied him as he maneuvered the car. He might have offered her a ride, but he certainly didn't seem happy about it. His lips were pursed, and his forehead creased in a frown. Although traffic was heavy and sluggish, that didn't seem to be the reason for his impatience. She assumed it had something to do with her.

Jayne folded her hands in her lap, regretting that she'd accepted his invitation. She couldn't understand why he'd offer her a ride when her presence was clearly upsetting to him.

"You're quiet this morning," Riley commented, glancing her way.

"I was afraid to say anything." Jayne focused her gaze on her laced fingers. "You looked like you'd bite my head off if I did."

"When has that ever stopped you?"

"Today."

Riley's frown grew, if anything, fiercer. "What made you think I was angry?"

"You look like you ate rattlesnakes for breakfast," she replied.

"I do? Now?"

A quick movement — what Jayne termed an "almost smile" — touched his mouth.

"Your face was all scrunched up," she said, "and your expression was terribly intense. I was wondering why you're giving me a ride when it's clear you don't want me in the car with you."

"Not want you in the car?" he repeated. "That's not it at all. I was just thinking about a problem . . . at the office."

"Then your thoughts must be deep and dark."

"They have been lately." His face softened as he averted his eyes from the traffic to briefly look at her. "Don't worry, I've never been one to do anything unless it's exactly what I want."

Pleased by his response, Jayne relaxed and smiled. Riley was different from anyone she'd known before. Yet in certain ways they were alike. He was at ease with her quiet manner. In the past Jayne had felt it necessary to make small talk with men. Doing that had been contrary to her nature; finding things to talk about was always difficult, even with Gloria. Mark would expect it, and she'd make the effort for his benefit.

Riley stopped at a red light, and Jayne watched as his fingers loosened their grip on the steering wheel. He turned to her. "You're looking better this morning."

"Like I said, I feel wonderful. It was probably the soup."

"Undoubtedly," Riley agreed with a crooked grin.

"Thank you again," she said shyly, astonished by how much a smile could alter a man's appearance. The glow in his blue eyes warmed Jayne as effectively as a ray of sunlight. "You mentioned an office. What do you do?"

The hesitation was so slight that Jayne thought she must have imagined it.

"I'm an inspector."

"For the city?" Somehow his words

didn't ring entirely true, but Jayne attributed that notion to reading too many thrillers and suspense novels.

"Yeah, for the city. I'll let you off at the next corner." Not waiting for her response, he switched lanes and stopped at the curb.

"I'm in your debt again," she murmured. Her hand closed over the door handle. "Thank you."

"Have a good day, Miss Prim and Proper."

Jayne flashed angry eyes at him. When she clenched her hands and stalked away, Riley grinned. Jayne Gilbert was easy to bait. Her reaction to teasing suggested she was an only child. That would also account for her quiet, independent nature. He appreciated that quality in her. Without realizing it, Riley smiled, his troubled thoughts vanishing in the face of a simple display of emotion. Who would've guessed a shy librarian could have that effect on him?

Jayne was watching the evening news two days later while a casserole baked in the oven, when Riley's image flitted into her restless mind. The news story relayed the unsavory details of a prostitution ring that had recently been broken. The blonde woman on the screen looked vaguely familiar, and Jayne wondered if she'd seen her that night in Soft Sam's, the night she met Riley. But she hadn't been wearing her glasses, and it was difficult to tell.

Jayne didn't know what made her think of Riley. She hadn't seen him for a few days. In fact, she'd been half looking for him. At first he'd made his views of her plain. Now she wasn't sure what he thought of her. Not that she expected to bowl him over with her natural beauty and charm. She didn't expect that from any man. She liked Riley, enjoyed his company, and that was rare. The fact was, Jayne didn't know what to make of her relationship with him. Perhaps it was premature to even call it a relationship. Friends — she hoped so. But nothing more. Riley wasn't the type of man she pictured walking into her class reunion. No, she'd reserve Mark for her classmates' inspection. Riley was too . . . rough-edged. Mark seemed smoother. More sociable.

Shaking her head, Jayne felt guilty that her thoughts about Riley — and Mark, for that matter — could be so self-serving. After all, Riley had gone out of his way for her.

On impulse, she pulled the steaming casserole from the oven and divided it into two equal portions. With giant oven mitts protecting her hands, she carried the steaming dish down the hallway to Riley's apartment. She knocked at the door, balancing the casserole in one hand, and waited impatiently for him to answer.

The door was jerked open in an angry motion, but his frown disappeared as soon as he saw her. "Jayne?"

"Hi." Now that she was there, she felt like an idiot, but she'd been behaving a lot like one lately. "The library got a new cookbook this week. I read through it and decided to try this recipe."

"And you're looking for a guinea pig?"

"No." The comment offended her. "I wanted to thank you for fixing me dinner the other night and for the ride to work."

"It isn't necessary to repay me."

Jayne sighed. "I know that. But I wanted to do this. Now are you going to let me in, or do I have to stand here while we argue?"

"I don't know — you look kind of appealing like that."

"I didn't think men found 'prim and proper' appealing." She loved turning his own words back on him.

Riley grinned, and his whole face relaxed with the movement. The dark blue eyes sparkled, and Jayne was reminded that he could be devastatingly attractive when he wanted to be.

"Prim and proper women can be fascinating," he said softly.

Jayne sucked in her breath. "Don't play with me, Riley. I'm not good at games. The only reason I'm here is to thank you."

"I should be thanking you — this smells delicious." He stepped aside, and Jayne brought the dish to his kitchen. Riley's apartment was similar to her own, although Riley possessed none of her sense of orderliness. His raincoat had been carelessly tossed over the back of a living room chair, and three days worth of newspapers littered the carpet.

"It's chicken tamale pie," she told him, feeling awkward without the dish in her hands.

"Will you join me?"

Jayne was convinced the invitation wasn't sincere until she remembered his claim that he never said or did anything without meaning it.

"No, my dinner is waiting for me. I just wanted —"

"— to thank me," he finished for her.

"No," she said mischievously. "I came to prove that prim and proper girls have talents you might not expect."

"Given half a chance, I'd say they'd take over the world."

"According to what I remember from Sunday school class, we're supposed to inherit it." She gave him a comical glance. "Or is that the meek and mild?"

"Never meek, Ms. Gilbert." Chuckling, Riley closed the door after her and sighed thoughtfully. He wasn't so sure Jayne was going to control the world as he'd teased, but he was genuinely concerned that he could be falling for her. And then, without much trouble, she'd end up ruling his heart and his life.

He swept a hand across his face, trying to wipe out the memory of her standing in his apartment. Instead, he realized how *right* it had felt to be with her, even if it was only for those few minutes. This woman was entering his life when he was least prepared to deal with it. He was in his thirties and cynical about the world. She was *much* too innocent for him, yet he found himself attracted to her. She touched a vulnerable part of him that Riley hadn't known existed, a softness he thought had vanished long ago.

For both their sakes, it would be best to avoid her.

Several times before her date with Mark, Jayne studied her dating advice books. With Gloria choosing her outfit, Jayne dressed casually, or what was casual for her — a plaid skirt and light sweater. She used lots of mascara and left her hair down. It fell in gentle waves to her shoulders and shone from repeated brushing. Re-reading *How to Get a Man Interested in You* while she waited, Jayne mentally reviewed the discussion topics Gloria had given her and recalled her friend's tips on how to keep a conversation going. She hoped Mark would do most of the talking and all that would be required of her was to smile and bat her eyelashes. Granted, that felt a bit false, but she was starting to believe that social interactions, especially male-female ones, often were.

Mark arrived precisely when he said he would. Their evening together went surprisingly well. And fortunately she was farsighted so she had no trouble seeing the screen, even without her glasses. The movie was a comedy with slapstick humor.

After the movie, Mark suggested a cup of coffee.

Jayne agreed, and her hand slid automatically inside her pocket to the list of conversation ideas. But she didn't need them. Mark was a nice man with a huge ego. He spoke in astonishing detail about his position as an office manager. She didn't know why he felt the need to impress her with his importance, but as the books suggested, she fawned over every word, exhausting though that was.

In return she told him she worked for the city, but not in what capacity. Librarians were stereotyped. It didn't matter that she fit that stereotype perfectly. Later, as they went back to her apartment, Jayne thought wryly that Gloria needn't have worried about making up a list of topics to discuss. As she'd originally hoped, Mark had done most of the talking. She should've been relieved, even pleased, but she wasn't. With Mark she felt like . . . like an accessory.

Outside her apartment door, clenching her keys, Jayne looked up at him. "I had a lovely time. Thank you, Mark."

He placed his hand on the wall behind her and lowered his head. Jayne felt a second of apprehension. She wasn't sure she wanted him to kiss her. Nonetheless, she closed her eyes as his mouth settled over hers for a gentle kiss. Pleasant, but not earth-shattering. "Can I see you again?" he asked, his breath fanning her temple.

"Ah . . . sure."

"How about dinner Wednesday night? Do you like to dance?"

"Love to," she told him, wondering how quickly a book and CD could teach her. She had about as much rhythm as a piece of lint. The class reunion was bound to have some kind of dancing, and she'd need to learn sooner or later, anyway. She'd check out an instruction book and CD on Monday. Her motto should be *By the Book,* she decided with a satisfied grin.

Monday afternoon, when she was walking home from the bus stop, she heard Riley call her from the parking lot across the street.

"Hello," Jayne called and waved back, feeling unreasonably pleased at seeing him again. He carried his raincoat over his arm, and she wondered if he ever wore the silly thing. She'd only seen it on him once or twice, yet he had it with him constantly.

Checking both sides of the street before jogging across, Riley joined her in front of the apartment building and smiled roguishly when he noted the CDs poking out of her bag. "Don't tell me the books on man-hunting didn't help and you're advancing to audio?"

Jayne studied the sidewalk between her shoes. "No, Mark asked me to go dancing, and . . . I'm not very good at it."

"Two left feet aren't uncommon." Riley resisted the urge to fit his hand under her chin and lift her gaze to his. He wanted to pull her hair free of that confining clasp and run his fingers through it. The thought irritated him. He didn't want to feel these things. This woman was like a red light flashing *trouble.* She didn't hide her desire to get married, or at least find a man, while Riley had no intention of settling down. Yet he was like a moth fluttering dangerously close to that very same light. The light warning there was trouble ahead . . .

"I went to a few dances in high school, but that was years ago," Jayne said. "Ten, to be exact, and I don't remember much. I don't think just shuffling my feet around will work this time."

"Do you want any help?" The offer slid from his mouth before he could censor it. Silently he cursed himself.

"Help?" Jayne repeated, surprised. "You'd do that?"

He nodded. Yes, he'd do that, just so she'd marry this Mark guy and get out of his life. He sighed. Who was he trying to kid? He'd do it so he could stop wondering how she'd feel in his arms.

"It *would* be easier with a partner,"

Jayne murmured. She saw Riley's eyebrows drawn together in a dark glower as if he already regretted making the offer. "If you're sure."

"I'll be at your place in an hour."

"Let me cook dinner, then . . . as a means of thanking you," she added hurriedly.

This cozy scene was going to be difficult enough as it was. "Another time," he said, putting her off gently.

Calling himself every kind of fool, Riley knocked on Jayne's apartment door precisely one hour later. He'd never felt more mixed up in his life. His arms ached for the warm feel of this woman, and yet at the same time he dreaded what that sensation would do to him.

Jayne opened the door, and Riley mumbled something under his breath as he stalked past. She couldn't understand what he was saying. She'd changed out of her "uniform" and into linen pants the color of summer wheat and a soft cashmere sweater. The instruction book that came with the CD was open on the coffee table.

"You ready?" Riley's voice had a definite edge to it.

"Yes, of course," she said too quickly, turning on the CD player. "The first part is a guide to waltzing. The book says . . ." Feeling ridiculous, Jayne placed her hands on her hips and boldly met his scowl. "Listen, Riley, I appreciate the offer, but you don't have to do this."

"I thought you wanted to learn how to dance."

"I do, but with a willing partner. From the looks you're giving me, one would assume you're furious about the whole idea."

Indecision showed in every weather-beaten feature of his face. "I don't want you to get the wrong impression, Jayne. I'm rotten husband material."

She valued his honesty. He wasn't interested in her, not romantically. They hadn't even gone out on a date. He didn't think of her in those terms, yet he'd made an effort to seek her out, talk to her, be with her. If he wanted to be just friends, it was fine with her. In fact, wasn't friendship what *she* preferred, too? "I think I realized that from the first time I saw you in the elevator. You'd make some poor girl a terrible husband, Riley Chambers. What I don't understand is why you've appointed yourself my

116

fairy godfather."

A slow smile crept into his eyes. "If you turned into a pumpkin at midnight, that might be the best thing all the way around."

"You don't know your fairy tales very well, Mr. Chambers. The coach turned back into a pumpkin. Not Cinderella."

The sweet sounds of a Viennese waltz swirled around them. An instructor's voice rang out. "Gentlemen. Place one hand on the lady's waist . . ."

Riley bowed elegantly. "Shall we?"

Pretending to fan her face, Jayne batted her lashes and gave him a demure look. "Why, Rhett, you have the most charmin' manner."

Loosely Riley took Jayne in his arms. She followed his lead, and he could tell by the concentration on her face that this was difficult for her. "*One,* two, three. *One,* two, three," the instructor's voice chanted.

"Pretend you're enjoying yourself," he told her, "otherwise Mark's going to think you're in pain."

Jayne laughed involuntarily. She *was* trying too hard. "Don't be so anxious for me to step on your toes."

"I'm not!" Riley positioned his hands so the need to touch her was at a minimum. He adjusted his fingers at her shoulder and then at her hip, all to no avail. Each time his hands shifted, he became aware of the warmth that lay just beneath his fingertips. He tried desperately not to notice.

Swallowing, he concentrated on moving to the music and held his breath. Fairy godfather indeed! He should be arrested for the thoughts that were racing at breakneck speed through his head. This entire situation was ridiculous. Riley had held women far more intimately than he was embracing Jayne, and yet he was acting like a teenage boy on his first date. Briefly he wondered if she had any suspicion of what she was doing to him. He doubted it; knowing Jayne, she'd have to read about it first. Or maybe she had. Maybe this whole thing was an experiment, just like her visit to Soft Sam's. Gritting his teeth, Riley did his utmost to ignore the feel and the flowery scent of the woman in his arms — to ignore the texture of her soft skin, the way her body moved in perfect rhythm with his.

Jayne nodded happily to the music. *One,* two, three . . . This was going so much better than she'd imagined. Riley was obviously a good dancer, moving confidently with a grace she wouldn't have expected in a man his size. She felt a warmth where he positioned his hands at her waist, and forced her body to relax.

"How am I doing?" she asked after a while.

"Fine," he muttered. He was more convinced than ever that Jayne had no idea what she was doing to him. He had to endure this torture, so he'd do it with a smile. "When you go out with Mark, do you plan to leave your hair up?" He inched back to put some distance between them.

"Probably not."

"Then maybe you should let it

down now. You know, to . . . uh, practice." He couldn't believe he was suggesting this, well aware that he was only making things worse.

"Okay." She reached up and took off the clasp; the dark length fell free.

"What about your glasses?" he asked next, resisting the urge to lift a strand of hair and feel its texture.

"Mark has never seen me in glasses."

"Then take them off."

"All right." She laid her glasses beside the hair clasp on the end table. A fuzzy, blurred Riley smiled down at her.

"No squinting."

"I can't see you close up."

"You won't see Mark, either, so it shouldn't make any difference."

"True," she agreed. But it *did* make

a difference. She didn't need her glasses or anything else to know it was Riley's arms around her. When she slid into his embrace once again, it felt completely natural. His hold on her tightened ever so slightly, and when he pressed his jaw against the side of her neck, Jayne's eyes slowly closed. They danced, and she observed that they fit together perfectly.

Riley drew her closer, and Jayne's mind whirled with a confused mixture of emotions. She shouldn't be feeling this. Not with Riley. But she didn't want to question it, not now. . . .

"This feels good," she whispered, fighting the impulse to trace the rugged line of his jaw. He smelled wonderful, a blend of spicy aftershave and — what? Himself, she decided.

Riley smoothed her hair, letting his hand glide down the silky length from the crown of her head to her shoulder. Reluctantly he stopped when the last notes of the waltz faded away.

"Yes, it does feel good," Riley said, his voice husky. *Too good,* his mind added.

He dropped his arms, and Jayne thrilled at his hesitancy when he stepped back. "I don't think you'll have any problems with the waltz."

"I shouldn't have," she said. "Anyway, with Mark all I need to do is look at him with adoring eyes and bat my lashes, and he's happy."

Riley didn't like the idea of Jayne flirting with another man. He knew that didn't make sense, since he was helping her prepare for a date with this Mark guy. "That won't satisfy a man for long," he muttered.

"It'll satisfy Mark," she countered. "I'm not exactly a flirt, you know. I'm not even sure how most women do it."

"It seems to me you're doing a good job learning."

"What do you mean?"

"Just now — dancing. You were practically throwing yourself at me."

"I was not!"

"You sure were."

Jayne was too humiliated to argue. She vaulted across the room and removed the CD. Her hands shook as she returned it to the plastic case. "That was an awful thing to say."

"It's about time you woke up and realized what men are like."

"I've already told you I don't need

a fairy godfather."

"You need *someone* to tell you the score."

Jayne glared at him angrily. "And I suppose you're the one to enlighten me."

"Yup. Someone has to. You can't go flaunting yourself the way you just did with me."

"Flaunting?" Jayne almost choked on the word.

"That's right — flaunting." Riley hated himself for the things he was saying. He was both furious and unreasonable — a bad combination.

"*You* were the one who offered to show me how to dance. I . . . I even told you —"

"You can't tease a man, Jayne," he interrupted, coming to grips with his emotions. "Not me, not Mark, not any man."

"And how many times do I have to tell you I'm not a tease? Honestly, look at me!"

"That's the problem. I *am* looking."

"And?" she whispered, shocked at the tightness of his voice.

"And . . ." He hesitated. "All I can think about is doing this." He reached for her, taking her in his arms and covering her mouth with his.

Jayne was too stunned to react. The kiss had the sweetest, most tantalizing effect, momentarily causing her to forget the angry censure in his voice.

Regaining her composure — or pretending to — she broke away. "What made you do that?"

The look he was giving her told Jayne he wasn't pleased about that kiss. "I don't know. It was a mistake."

"I . . . yes." And yet Jayne didn't want to think of it that way.

"You go out with Mark, and we'll leave it at that."

"But —"

"Just go out with him, Jayne."

She dropped her gaze to the carpet. "All right."

Four

After she'd buzzed Gloria in, Jayne jerked open the apartment door. "What took you so long? Mark's due any minute."

Flustered, Gloria shook her head. "If you weren't so afraid to wear your glasses, you'd see exactly what he looks like."

Being the good friend she was, Gloria had volunteered to be there when Mark arrived so she could tell Jayne if he'd be an acceptable date for the high school reunion. Mark's image remained a bit fuzzy in her mind, but as the day of her reunion drew closer, Jayne discovered how badly she wanted to go. But she'd decided early on not to attend without a handsome man at her side. The problem was that Mark was her only likely prospect. And she didn't even know if he'd be interested!

"You look fantastic," Gloria commented, stepping back to examine Jayne's outfit. "Are you sure you can dance in that?"

Jayne had wondered the same thing. The silk blouse was new, pale blue with a pleated front. The black skirt was standard straight fare, part of her everyday uniform. She'd spent what seemed like hours on her hair, but to no avail. It was too straight and thick to manage. In the end, she'd tied it at the base of her neck with a chiffon scarf that was a shade deeper than her blouse.

"I shouldn't have any trouble dancing." But then she hadn't graduated beyond the waltzing stage. Riley had left soon after their kissing fiasco, and she hadn't seen him since. Every time Jayne thought about what had happened, she grew angry . . . not with Riley, but with herself. She hadn't meant to flirt with him, but she wasn't so naive that she didn't know what was happening. Pride had demanded that she pretend otherwise. But she regretted the kiss. It had been so wonderful that four days later the warm taste of his mouth still lingered on hers. Nor could she erase the sensation of being held in his arms.

"You're sure I look okay?" Jayne

raised questioning eyes to her friend. As it was, she had to drum up enthusiasm for this date.

"You look fine."

"Before, it was fantastic."

"Fantastic, then."

Straightening the chiffon scarf at her neck, Jayne closed her eyes. She had a bad feeling about tonight. If she was honest, she'd admit she'd rather be going with Riley. She felt comfortable with him. Except, of course, for that kiss. And it'd been . . . not comfortable but exciting. Memorable. However, Riley hadn't spoken to her in days. She wasn't entirely sure he even liked her; the signals she'd received from him were conflicting. It was almost as though he didn't want to be attracted to her but couldn't resist.

The buzzer went, and she cast a frantic glance in Gloria's direction and quickly tucked her glasses inside her purse.

"Calm down," Gloria said. "You're going to have a wonderful time."

"Tell me why I don't believe that," Jayne mumbled on her way to the door.

Riley Chambers pressed the button on his remote control to change channels. He'd seen fifteen-second segments of no fewer than ten shows. Nothing held his interest, and there was no point trying to distract himself. Jayne was on his mind again. Only she didn't flit in and out of his thoughts the way she had before. Tonight she was a constant presence, taunting him. Television wasn't going to help; neither was reading or the internet or any other diversion he could invent.

Standing, Riley paced to the window to stare at the rain-soaked street. He buried his hands in his pockets. So she was going out with this Mark character. Dinner and dancing. He shouldn't care. But he did. The idea of another man with his arms around Jayne disturbed him. It more than disturbed him, it made him completely crazy.

She'd felt so good in his arms. Far better than she had any right to. Days later, he still couldn't banish the feel, the taste, the smell of her from his mind. Avoiding her hadn't worked. Nothing had. She lived three doors down from him, yet she might as well have packed her bags and moved into his apartment. She was there every minute of every night and he didn't like it. What he really wanted to do was exorcise her from his life. Cast those honey-brown eyes from his memory and go about his business the way he was paid to do. *No.* He turned. What he really wanted to do was find out what Mark was like.

Before he could analyze this insanity, he grabbed his raincoat and stormed out the door.

"Hello, Mark." Jayne greeted him with a warm smile. "I'd like to introduce my friend Gloria."

"Hello, Gloria." Mark stepped forward to shake Gloria's hand, then held it far longer than necessary. His eyes caressed her face until Jayne noticed the pink color in her friend's cheeks.

"It's nice meeting you." Gloria pulled her hand free. "But I have to be going."

"No," Jayne objected. "Really, Gloria, stay."

Gloria threw her a look that could have boiled water. "No. You and Mark are going out. Remember?" The last word was issued through clenched teeth.

"The more the merrier, I always say." Mark was staring at Gloria with obvious interest, or what Jayne assumed was interest. She couldn't really tell without her glasses.

"No, I have to go," Gloria insisted.

"That's a shame," Mark said.

There was another knock at the door, and three faces glared at it.

"I'll get that," Jayne said, excusing

135

herself. The few steps across the floor had never seemed so far. It could only be a neighbor, yet she wasn't expecting anyone. Least of all Riley.

"Riley." She breathed his name in a rush of excitement.

His gaze flew past her to Mark and Gloria. "I stopped by —" he paused, suddenly realizing he had to come up with a plausible excuse for his unexpected arrival "— to get the recipe for the casserole you made the other night. It was delicious," he said.

"Of course. Come in, please." Jayne stepped aside, trying to disguise her reaction, and Riley strolled past her.

"Riley Chambers, this is Mark Bauer and Gloria Bailey." Somehow she made it through the introductions without revealing her pleasure at Riley's unexpected visit.

"Pleased to meet you," Mark said stiffly, and the two men shook hands.

"Gloria." Riley nodded in the direction of Jayne's friend.

"Riley lives down the hall from me," Jayne felt obliged to add. "Gloria and I work together," she explained.

Riley nodded.

"I'll get you that recipe," Jayne told him.

"I'll help," Gloria said hurriedly, following her into the kitchen. "What's going on?" Gloria whispered the minute they were out of sight.

"I don't know."

"You don't really think he cares about that stupid recipe, do you?"

Jayne thought back to all the times she'd been with Riley. He bewildered her. He'd come to the library intent on harassing her, then had looked after her when she was ill. Most surprising had been his willingness to teach her to dance — which had turned into a scene that wouldn't soon be forgotten by either of them.

"With Riley, I never know."

"He's here to check out Mark."

Jayne's eyes widened with doubt. "I have trouble believing that."

"Trust me, kiddo, the guy's interested."

"Two men at the same time? The girls of St. Mary's would keel over if they knew." Two men interested in her was a slight exaggeration. The minute Mark had met Gloria he couldn't stop looking at her.

"What are you going to do?" Gloria wanted to know.

"What do you mean?"

"From the look of things, Riley isn't leaving."

Jayne bit her bottom lip. "What should I do, invite him along?"

"Invite us both."

"But what will Mark think?"

"It won't matter. The way Riley's giving him the evil eye, Mark's not likely to risk life and limb by asking you out again."

"Oh, I can't believe this."

"Where's that cookbook?" Gloria whispered, glancing into the living room.

There wasn't any point in looking. "I returned it last week."

"Then tell him that, for heaven's sake!"

Back in the living room, Jayne found the two men sitting on the sofa, staring at each other like angry bears. It was as if one had invaded the other's territory.

Riley stood. Slowly Mark followed suit.

"I'm sorry, Riley, but I returned that book to the library. I'll see if I can pick it up for you, if you'd like."

"Please."

Gloria stepped forward, linking her hands together. "Jayne and I were just thinking that since the four of us are all here maybe we could go out together."

Jayne nodded. "Right," she said boldly. "We were."

"Not dancing." Riley categorically dismissed that.

"There's a new movie at the Lloyd Center," Gloria suggested.

"A movie would be fun." Jayne nodded, looking at Mark. After all, he was supposed to be her date. "We could always eat later."

"That sounds fine," Mark agreed with little enthusiasm.

For that matter, eagerness for this impromptu double date was remarkably absent. The silence in Mark's car as they drove to the shopping complex grated on Jayne's fragile nerves. But she knew better than to even attempt a conversation.

At the theater Mark and Riley bought the popcorn while the two women found seats. The place was crowded and they ended up far closer to the front than Jayne liked.

"This isn't working," she whispered.

"You're telling me. The temperature in that car was below freezing."

"I know. What should I do?" Jayne

could hear the desperate appeal in her own voice.

"Nothing. Things will take care of themselves." Gloria sounded far more confident than Jayne felt.

The two men returned, and to her delighted surprise, Riley claimed the seat beside her. Mark took the one next to Gloria. The women glanced at each other and shared a sigh of relief. Apparently Mark and Riley had settled things in the theater lobby.

For his part, Riley wasn't pleased. His instincts told him Jayne was going to be hurt by this guy. He'd seen the looks Mark was giving Gloria. Three minutes in the lobby, and the two men had come to an agreement. Riley would sit with Jayne, Mark with Gloria. If Jayne was out to find herself a decent man, he thought grimly, Mark Bauer wasn't the one. She should look elsewhere.

The theater darkened, and after the previews the credits started to roll. Jayne squinted, then pulled her glasses out of her purse. It was ridiculous to pretend any longer. She doubted Mark had even noticed.

Before they'd entered the theater, Jayne hadn't paid much attention to the movie they were about to see. She soon realized it was going to be filled with blood and gore. She swallowed uncomfortably.

"What's wrong?" Riley whispered and grinned when he noticed she'd put her glasses back on.

"Nothing." She couldn't think of a way to tell him that any form of violence greatly upset her. She detested movies like this where men treated life cheaply, and grotesque horror was all part of an intriguing plot.

At the first gory scene, Jayne clutched the armrests until her fingers ached and closed her eyes, praying no one was aware of her odd behavior.

"Jayne?"

Riley's voice was so low she wasn't even sure she'd heard him. Opening her eyes, she turned to look at him. "Are you all right?" he asked solicitously.

With a weak smile, she nodded. A blast of gunfire rang from the screen, and she winced and shook her head.

"Do you want to leave?"

"No."

Watching her, Riley wasn't surprised that she was troubled by violence. It fit with what he knew of her — all part of the innocence he'd come to like so much, the goodness he'd come to count on. He didn't want to fall for her, but he knew the signs.

His interest in the movie waned. Her hand still clenched the armrest in a death grip, and with a gentleness he hardly knew he possessed, Riley pried her fingers loose and tucked her hand in his, offering her comfort. She turned to him with a look of such gratitude that it took years of hard-won self-control not to lean forward and kiss her. He didn't like this feeling. Now wasn't the time to get involved with a woman, especially *this* woman. It was too dangerous. For him and possibly for her.

■ ■ ■ ■

Thursday morning, Gloria was waiting for Jayne on the front steps of the library.

"Morning," Jayne muttered, feeling defeated. She'd been standing at the bus stop when Riley drove past. He hadn't even looked in her direction, and she'd felt as though a little part of her had died at the disappointment. "How did everything go with Mark?" Jayne's original date had taken Gloria home.

"Fine . . . I guess."

"Did he ask you out?"

"Yeah, but I'm not interested." Gloria wrapped her arms around her waist and shook her head. "I finally figured out what's wrong. Mark reminds me too much of my ex."

"Mark's off my list, as well."

"I would think so. Riley would probably skin him alive if he showed up at your door again."

"I don't understand Riley," Jayne murmured. "He barely even said good-night when he dropped me off. He wouldn't even look at me." And men claimed they didn't understand women! For all her intelligence, all the reading she'd done, Jayne was at a loss to explain Riley's strange behavior. She had thought they'd shared something special during that horrible movie, and then the minute they got outside, he treated her as though she had some contagious disease.

"Who would you rather go to the reunion with? Riley or Mark?"

Jayne didn't need to mull that over.

"Riley."

"Then you need to change tactics."

"Oh, Gloria, I don't know. You make this sound like some kind of game."

"Do you want to attend the reunion or not?"

"I do, but . . ."

"So, form your plan and choose your weapons."

Jayne might not have needed to ponder which man interested her most, but tactics were something else. She liked Riley, and she sensed that her feelings for him could grow a lot more intense. But the opposite side of the coin was the reality that if she chose to pursue a relationship with this man, she could be hurt.

That evening, still undecided about what to do, Jayne was surprised to receive a call from Mark, asking her out again. Apparently the man didn't scare off as easily as Gloria and Riley seemed to think. Or it could be that Mark had noticed Riley's lack of interest following the movie. It didn't matter; she politely declined.

When she didn't see Riley the following day, either, Jayne was convinced he was avoiding her again. Only this time she was armed with ammunition and reinforcement from Gloria.

That evening, Jayne made another casserole from the Mexican cookbook — which she'd taken out again — and delivered it to Riley's door.

Surprise etched fine lines around his eyes when Riley answered her knock.

"Hello." Jayne forced a bright smile.

He frowned, obviously not pleased to see her.

"I brought you dinner." It had all sounded so simple when she'd discussed her plans with Gloria earlier in the day. Now her stomach felt as though a weight had settled there, and her resolve was weakening more every minute. "It's another casserole from the same cookbook you asked about the other night."

His hand remained on the door. "You didn't need to do that."

"I wanted to." Her smile was about to crumple. "You mentioned it the night Mark was by. . . . You do remember, don't you?" He still hadn't asked her into his apartment. She wasn't any good at this flirting business. Chagrined, she dropped her gaze to the floor. "I can see you're busy, so I'll just leave this with you."

Reluctantly he stepped aside.

Rarely had Jayne been more miserable. Things weren't supposed to happen like this. According to Gloria, Riley would appreciate her efforts and gratefully ask her to join him.

She moved into his kitchen and saw the box from a frozen microwave dinner sitting on the counter.

After setting the casserole on the stove she removed her oven mitts. "Don't worry about returning the baking dish." She didn't want him thinking she was looking for more excuses to see him. She had been, but that didn't matter anymore. Embarrassed and ill at ease, she gave him a weak smile. "Enjoy your dinner."

"Jayne." His hand on her shoulder stopped her, and when she raised her eyes to his, he pulled away, thrusting his fingers into his hair. "I wish you hadn't done this."

"I know," she said and swallowed miserably. "I won't again. I . . . I don't know what I did to make you so upset with me, but your message is coming through loud and clear."

"Jayne, listen. I saw those books you're reading. I'm not the man for you. I told you already — I'd make a terrible husband." He took a step toward her.

"Husband!" she spat. "I'm not looking for a husband."

"Then what *do* you want?" He knew his voice was raised, he couldn't help it. Jayne did that to him. He saw the tears in her eyes and watched as she tried to blink them away. "Then why are you reading those ridiculous books?" he asked.

With her fists clenched, Jayne met his glare. "I have my reasons."

"No doubt." The proud tilt of her chin tore at his heart. He didn't know what Jayne thought she was doing, but if she was serious about a relationship with him, the timing couldn't be worse. The dangers of this undercover assignment were many and real. He had enough to worry about without having his head messed up by a woman. But Jayne wasn't an ordinary woman. He'd known it the first time she'd flared back at him. She was genuine and sweet and, yes, naive. She was also smart and he sensed the passion beneath her demure exterior.

"What you think of me is irrelevant," she said, flexing her hands at her sides. "If you must know, all I really want is to attend my high school reunion. And I'm going even if I have to hire a man to go with me." Her voice rose with every word. "And furthermore, I'm going to learn to dance, and if you won't help me, fine. I'll find someone else who will."

"So *that's* what this is all about? And the casserole is in exchange for dancing lessons?" No way was he addressing the issue of a hired companion. But at least she hadn't mentioned Mark Bauer.

"Yes."

"Fine." He walked across the room and flipped on the radio. Soft music filled the apartment. "Come on, let's dance, if that's all you want."

The invitation held as much welcome as cold charity. Jayne's first response was to throw his offer back in his face, but she managed to swallow her pride. After all, finding a way into his arms was exactly the reason she'd come here tonight.

When she walked into his embrace, he held her stiffly. His tense muscles kept her away from him, so there was only minimal contact.

"You didn't hold me like this the other day," she protested.

Gritting his teeth, Riley brought her closer into his arms. Eyes shut, he breathed in the scent of her hair. She reminded him of springtime, fresh and eager and so unbelievably trusting that it frightened him.

His hands sought her hair. Silky, glorious, just as he'd known it would be. He removed the clasp and let it fall to the floor. His fingers tangled with her hair as a tenderness for the woman enveloped him.

The music changed to an upbeat song with a bubbly rhythm, but their steps remained unchanged. Dancing was only an excuse to hold each other, and they both knew it.

Riley wrapped his arms around her. Their feet barely shifted as the pretense lost its purpose.

Jayne's arms were tight around his neck. She didn't dare move for fear her actions would break this magical spell. There was something strong and powerful about Riley that she couldn't resist. Her mouth found his neck, and her warm breath left a film of moisture against his skin. Lightly she kissed him there.

Riley stiffened, his whole body tensing at her seemingly playful kiss.

"Jayne," he breathed. "What are you trying to do to me?"

"The same thing you're doing to me," she answered. Her own voice was weak. "I've never felt like this before. . . ."

The only response he seemed capable of was a groan.

"Riley, kiss me," she said urgently. "Please kiss me."

He angled her head to one side and slanted his mouth over hers with a desperate hunger that burned in him like a raging fire.

He kissed her again with an intensity that drove him beyond his will. His mouth sought hers until they were both weak and trembling.

"Jayne," he whispered harshly, "tell me to leave you alone. Tell me to stop."

"But I like it."

"Don't say that."

"But, Riley, it feels so good. *You* feel so good."

"Jayne," he pleaded, wanting her to stop him. Instead she arched into him, her mouth on his.

"I want to kiss you forever," she whispered.

"Don't tell me that," he said, fighting with everything that was in him and losing the battle with every breath he took.

Instinctively she moved against him, and Riley thought he'd die with the pleasure and pain. He lowered his hands to her waist. "No more of that. Understand?"

"I don't think I do. I never dreamed anything could feel this wonderful."

Riley didn't even hear her as he

pressed his mouth to her cheek, her ear, her hair, anyplace but her lips.

"Jayne," he said a moment later. "We have to stop." He pressed his cheek to hers. His eyes were closed, and his breathing was labored as he struggled within himself.

Jayne moved so that her mouth found his, tasting, licking and kissing him until Riley feared she'd drive him mad.

"No more," he said harshly, breaking the contact. He held her away at arm's length, clasping her shoulder. "What's the matter with you?"

Jayne blinked.

"You're acting like a child with a new toy you've just discovered."

"But it feels so good." How flimsy that sounded, even to her.

"And just where did you think this

kissing and touching would end?"

"I thought . . ." She didn't know what she thought.

Riley looked down into Jayne's bewildered face and cursed the anger in his voice. "Listen, maybe you'd better find someone else for these lessons you're so keen to learn."

Jayne swallowed down the hurt. She didn't consider Riley her teacher. She'd believed they were exploring those exquisite sensations together. Her face felt hot with shame.

"Maybe I should!" she cried. "I'm sure Mark would be willing."

"Oh, no, you don't. Not with Mark."

"Who then? It isn't like I've got hordes of admirers lined up, dying to go out with me." Dramatically, she flung out her arm.

"That's not my problem." He attempted a show of indifference. "Find whoever you want. Just stay away from me."

"Don't worry." After this humiliation, she had no intention of ever seeing him again.

She couldn't get out of his apartment fast enough. Once inside her own, she felt tears of hurt and anger burning for release. They rolled down her face, despite all her efforts to hold them back.

Sinking into the soft cushion of her sofa, she buried her face in her hands. She was a twenty-seven-year-old virgin, hurrying to catch up with life, and it had backfired. She'd behaved like an irresponsible idiot just as Riley had claimed.

A loud knock sounded on the apartment door.

Aghast, she stared at it. There wasn't anyone in the world she wanted to see right now.

"Jayne!" Riley shouted. "Open up. I know you're in there."

She was too shocked to move. Riley was the last person she expected to come to her now.

Riley gave a disgusted sigh. "The choice is yours. Either open that door, or I'll kick it down."

His threat was convincing enough to prompt her to unlatch the lock and open the door.

Riley stood in front of her and handed her the oven mitts. "You forgot these."

Wordlessly she took them.

The guilt he felt at the sight of her red eyes knotted his stomach. "I think we'd better talk."

Like a robot, she moved aside. Riley stalked past her and into the apartment. "You want to attend that reunion? Fine. I'll take you."

"Why?"

"Haven't you ever heard that expression about not looking a gift horse in the mouth?"

"But why?"

"Because!" he shouted.

"That's not a reason."

"Well, it'll have to do."

FIVE

The glorious June sunshine splashed over the street, silhouetting the Burnside Bridge that towered above Riverside Park. The Saturday market was in full swing, and noisy crowds wandered down the busy street. Some gathered to watch a banjo player while others strolled past, their arms heavy with a variety of newly discovered treasures.

Jayne nibbled on a cinnamon-covered "elephant ear" pastry as she strolled from one booth to the next. Riley was at her side, carrying the shopping bag that grew increasingly heavy with every stop.

"I can't believe you've lived in Portland all these months and you didn't know about the Saturday market," she remarked.

"You do most of your shopping here?"

"Just the produce." Jayne offered him a bite of her elephant ear. "They're good, aren't they?"

Chewing, Riley nodded. "Delicious."

Finishing it off, Jayne brushed the sugar from her fingers and dumped the napkin in the garbage. Riley took her hand and smiled. "Where to next?"

"The fish market. I want to try a new salmon recipe." They strolled down the wide street to the vendor who displayed fresh fish laid out on a bed of crushed ice.

"I didn't know it was legal to catch salmon this small," Riley commented as the vendor wrapped up Jayne's choice.

"That's a rainbow trout," she said and laughed.

"I thought you said you were buying salmon."

"I changed my mind. The trout looked too good to resist."

"At the moment, so do you."

His lazy voice reached through the noisy crowd to touch her heart. Tears filled her eyes, and she quickly looked away, not wanting him to see the effect his words had on her.

The stout vendor handed Riley the fish, and he tucked it in the brown shopping bag. Before his attention returned to her, Jayne brushed the tears from her cheek.

"Jayne." Concern was evident in his tone. "What's wrong?"

She smiled up at him through her happiness. "No one's ever said things like that to me."

"Like what?" His brow compressed.

"That I'm irresistible."

"My sweet little librarian," he said, placing an arm around her shoulders, drawing her close to his side. "You tie me up in knots a sailor couldn't undo."

"Oh, Riley, do I really?" She felt excruciatingly pleased. "I owe you so much."

Despite his efforts not to, Riley frowned. He was grateful that Jayne didn't seem to notice. He wondered how this virtuous librarian, whom he'd once thought of as a prim and proper young woman, could inspire such desire in him. Over the years, he'd been with a number of women. None of them compared to her. None of them had meant to him what she did. At night, unable to sleep, he often lay awake imagining Jayne. This woman tugged, like a swift undercurrent, at his senses. Jayne in bed, soft and mussed, her hair spilling over the pillow. The image of her was so strong that it was a constant battle not to make it real. The intensity of his feelings for her shocked him even now, weeks after having accepted her into his life. This wasn't the time to be caught up with a woman. Losing sight of his assignment could be dangerous. It could cost him his life. But if he hadn't acted when he did, he could have lost *her,* and that thought was intolerable. As soon as this job was over, he was getting out. The time had come to think about settling down. Jayne had done that to him, and he realized for the first time how much he wanted the very lifestyle he'd previously shunned.

Therein lay the problem. Being with her had placed a burden on him. She made him ache with need; at the same time, he experienced the overpowering urge to protect her. This was a dilemma — because there was no one to protect her from him but his own conscience. The weight of that responsibility fell heavily on his shoulders.

"You're very quiet," Jayne commented when they reached the parked car. "Is something wrong?"

"No." He smiled down on her and was instantly drawn into those warm brown eyes.

"I'm glad you came with me."

Riley had to admit he looked for excuses to be with her. Carrying her bags was one, offering her a ride was another. Simple things to do, but they brought him pleasure out of all proportion to the effort they entailed.

They drove back to the apartment building in companionable silence. After parking in his assigned spot, Riley carried her purchases into the building.

"Will you come in?" she asked outside her door.

"Only for a minute."

Setting the shopping bags on the kitchen counter, Riley watched the subtle grace with which she moved around her small kitchen. "I'll have a surprise for you later," she announced.

"Dinner?"

"No. Not that." Every time Riley kissed her, he ended up pulling the clasp from her hair. Her surprise was an appointment with the hairdresser to restyle her hair so that when Riley held her again, he could do whatever he liked with it. "You'll have to come by this evening and see."

"I'll do that."

"Riley?" She turned to him and leaned against the counter, hands behind her back.

He looked at her intent face. "Hmm?"

"May I kiss you?"

"Now?" He swallowed; she didn't make keeping his hands off her easy.

"Please."

"Jayne, listen . . ."

"Okay." She moved to his side and slipped her arms over his chest to link her fingers behind his neck. Her soft body conformed to the hardness of his.

Riley groaned, finding it nearly impossible to maintain his resolve. He was convinced that she had no idea of the powerful effect she had on him.

"Do you like this?" She pressed her lips to his, and Riley felt his legs weaken. He was grateful for the support of the kitchen counter.

"Yes," he groaned.

She began to kiss him again, straining upward on her toes, but Riley quickly took charge. He kissed her with the hunger that ate at his insides.

Jayne moved restlessly against him, but he broke away.

"No," he said abruptly, his chest heaving. "That's enough."

Jayne hung her head as the heat of embarrassment colored her cheeks. "I'm sorry, Riley."

"Think next time, will you? I'm not some high school kid for you to experiment with. I told you that before." He hated to see the hurt he was inflicting on her, but she didn't seem to understand the stress she was putting him under.

Jayne took a step backward.

He plowed his fingers through his hair. "I'll talk to you later. Okay?"

"Sure."

The door closed, and Jayne winced. Oh, dear, she was doing everything wrong. Riley wanted to cool things down just when she wanted to really heat them up for the first time in her life. Several men had kissed her over the years, but she'd never responded to any of them the way she did to Riley. He didn't merely light a spark; Riley Chambers ignited a bonfire within her. Jayne was as surprised as anyone. She'd thought she was too refined, too shy, trapped with too many hang-ups to experience the very physical desires Riley evoked in her. He'd taught her differently, and now she was riding a roller coaster, speeding downhill ahead of him. If it wasn't so ironic, she'd laugh.

Listening to the radio, Jayne finished putting away the morning's purchases. She changed clothes for her hair appointment and left the apartment soon after one. The beauty salon was a good mile away, but the day was gloriously warm, and she decided to walk instead of taking the bus. She wanted time to think.

As she strolled along, it seemed as if the whole world was alive. She saw and heard things that had passed her notice only weeks before. Birdsong filled the air, as did the laughter of children in the park.

Jayne cut a path through the lush green boulevard, pausing to watch several children swooping high on the park swings. She recognized a little girl from the library's story hour and waved as she continued down the meandering walkway.

Looking both ways before crossing the street, Jayne's gaze fell on Soft Sam's. She gave an involuntary shudder as she remembered the desperation of that first visit. She'd been so naive, thinking that because the place was in her neighborhood it would fulfill her requirements. Now she couldn't believe she'd even gone inside. She could just imagine what Riley had thought when he first saw her there. He'd warned her about the bar several times since, but he needn't have bothered. People went into Soft Sam's with one thing on their minds, and it wasn't companionship.

Jayne started across the street, and as she stepped off the curb, Riley came into view. He was standing in the doorway of Soft Sam's. She raised her arm, then paused, not knowing if she should call out to him or not. Before she could decide, a tall blonde woman joined him, slipping an arm through his and smiling boldly up at him. Her face was familiar, and it took Jayne several troubled seconds to realize the woman was the same one she'd seen on the evening news.

The hand she'd raised fell lifelessly to her side. Jayne felt as though someone had kicked her in the stomach. The numbing sensation of shock and disbelief moved up her arms and legs, paralyzing her for a moment.

A car horn blared, and she saw that she was standing in the middle of the street. Hurriedly she moved to the other side. Pausing to still her frantically beating heart, she rested her trembling hand on a fire hydrant for support.

Hadn't she just admitted the reason men and women went to a place like Soft Sam's? Riley was there now, and it wasn't his first visit. He could even be a regular customer. And from the looks that . . . that woman was giving him, they knew each other well.

The pain that went through her was white-hot, and her eyelids fluttered downward.

"Are you all right, miss?"

Jayne opened her eyes to find a police officer studying her, his face concerned.

"I'm fine. I . . . just felt dizzy for a minute."

The young man smiled knowingly. "You might want to check with a doctor."

"I will. Thank you, officer."

He touched the tip of his hat with his index finger. "No problem. You sure you'll be okay?"

"I'm sure."

With a determination that surprised even her, Jayne squared her shoulders and walked in the direction of the beauty salon. She'd read about men like Riley. If there was a blessing to be found in this, it was learning early on that there was another side to him. One that sought cheap thrills.

Her hand was on the glass door of the salon when she hesitated. She wasn't having her hair done for Riley, she told herself; she was doing it for the reunion. She wanted to go back looking different, didn't she? *None* of this was for Riley. None of it. It was for her.

Three hours later the reflection that greeted her in the salon mirror was hardly recognizable. Instead of thick, straight hair, soft, bouncy curls framed her face. Jayne stared back at her reflection and blinked. She looked almost pretty.

"What a difference," the hairdresser was saying.

"Yes," Jayne agreed. She paid the stylist and left a hefty tip. Anyone who could create the transformation this young woman had deserved a reward.

Jayne took the bus home. She sat staring out the side window, absorbed in what she'd witnessed earlier. For days she'd been planning this small surprise for Riley. Now she didn't care if she ever saw him again.

But perhaps that was a bit rash. If she was going to break things off, she'd wait until after the reunion. She knew she should be grateful to learn this about him, only she wasn't. The experience of undiluted love had been pure bliss.

Back inside her apartment, Jayne felt the need to talk to someone. She wouldn't mention what she'd seen. For that matter, she doubted she could put words to the emotions that simmered in her heart. She needed human contact so she wouldn't go crazy sitting here alone, thinking. She reached for the phone and called Gloria.

"Jayne, I'm so glad to hear from you," Gloria's voice boomed over the wire.

"Oh. Did something exciting happen?"

"I cannot believe my luck."

"You won the lottery!" It took effort to force some energy into her flat voice.

"Remember when you returned

those how-to books about meeting men to the library?"

Of course she did. When Riley had said he'd attend the reunion with her, she hadn't seen any reason to keep them.

"Well, guess who checked them out?"

"Who?" The answer was obvious.

"Me. And, Jayne, guess what? They work! I met this fantastic man in the Albertsons store today."

"At the grocery store?"

"Sure," Gloria said. "Remember how that one book says the supermarket on Saturdays is a great place to meet men? I met Lance in the frozen-food section."

"Congratulations."

"We're going to dinner tonight."

"That's great."

"I have a feeling about this man. He's everything I want. We even like the same things. Looking through our grocery carts, we discovered that we have identical tastes."

"I hate to rain on your parade," Jayne said, smiling for the first time. "But there's more to a compatible relationship than both of you liking broccoli."

"It's not only broccoli, but fish sticks and frozen orange juice. We even bought the same brand of microwave dinners."

The thought of cardboard meals reminded Jayne of Riley's haphazard eating patterns. She did her best to dispel all thoughts of him, with little success.

"I didn't mean to jabber on. You must've called for a reason."

"I just wanted to tell you about my hair."

"Oh, goodness, I was so excited about meeting Lance that I forgot. What does Riley think?"

"He hasn't seen it yet."

"All right, how do *you* feel about it?"

"It's . . . different."

"I knew it would be," Gloria said with a laugh.

"Listen, I've got to go. I'll talk to you Monday, and you can tell me all about your hot date." On second thought, it had been a mistake to phone Gloria. Jayne's mind was in turmoil, and she wondered if she'd made any sense at all.

"Okay, see you then."

After a few words of farewell, Jayne hung up.

Riley — she assumed it was him — knocked on her door at about seven. Jayne had known he'd come by, but she didn't have the nerve to confront him with what she'd seen. There wasn't anything she could say. The hurt was still too fresh and too poignant.

Careful not to make any noise, she sat reading a new mystery novel. She could immerse herself in fiction and forget for a time.

After three loud knocks he'd left, and she'd breathed easier.

Sunday morning she went out early and returned late. She couldn't avoid him forever, but she needed to put distance between them until she'd dealt with her emotions. When they did meet, she didn't want what she'd learned to taint her reactions.

185

■ ■ ■ ■

Early Monday afternoon Riley tossed an empty paper cup in the metal garbage can beside his desk. Jayne was avoiding him. He didn't blame her; he'd hurt her feelings by abruptly putting an end to their kissing. Someday, God willing, there wouldn't be any reason to stop. For now, he had to be in control and for more than the obvious reasons.

The report on his desk made him frown. He didn't like the sound of this. For that matter, he didn't like anything to do with Max Priestly. The man was a slimeball; Riley always felt as though he needed a shower after being around him. How anyone like Priestly had been elected to public office was beyond Riley.

Standing, he reached for his coat. He'd dealt with enough mud this weekend. He needed a break. Only he wasn't going to get it. He missed Jayne, missed her fresh, sweet scent and the way he felt about himself when he was with her. She brought out the best in him. For the first time in recent memory, he was being noble. Twice now he could have taken what she was so freely offering, and he hadn't. She didn't know or even appreciate his self-control, but in time she would. And he could wait.

A glance at his watch confirmed that he could probably catch her at the library. He'd take her to lunch and ease her embarrassment. There was always the possibility that Priestly would see them together, but it was a relatively small risk and one worth taking. Pulling on his raincoat, he walked out of the office.

His steps echoed on the floor of the main library as Riley made his way to the children's department. He stopped when he found Jayne. At first he didn't recognize her. She looked fabulous. A beauty. She was holding up a picture book to the children gathered around her on the floor.

One small boy raised his hand and said something Riley couldn't hear. Jayne reacted by laughing softly and shaking her head. Leaning forward, she spoke to the group of intent young faces.

Just watching her with those children made Riley's heart constrict. He loved this woman with a depth that astonished him. *Loved her.* The acknowledgment felt right and true.

Jayne closed the book, and the kids got up and surged closer, all chattering happily. Seeing her with these children created such intense desire in Riley that for a minute he couldn't breathe. Jayne was everything he could ever want. And a lot more than he deserved.

Gloria moved to Jayne's side and whispered in her ear. Instantly Jayne's gaze darted in Riley's direction. For a moment her eyes held a stricken look but that was quickly disguised. She stood, put the picture book down and said goodbye to the children, then walked over to him.

"Hello, Riley." Her voice held a note of hesitancy.

"Can I take you to lunch?"

She opened her mouth to tell him she'd already made other plans, when

Gloria intervened. "Go ahead," Gloria urged. "You haven't had lunch yet. And if you're a few minutes late, I'll cover for you."

There was nothing left for Jayne to do but agree.

Riley's gaze held hers. He wasn't sure he understood the message he found there. Jayne looked almost as though she was afraid of him, but he couldn't imagine why. "I like your hair."

Self-consciously she lifted her hand to the soft curls. "Thank you."

"Where would you like to eat?"

"Anywhere."

Her lack of enthusiasm was obvious. "Jayne, is something wrong?"

Her stricken eyes clashed with his. "No . . . how could there be?" Immediately her right eye began to twitch.

Riley argued with himself and decided not to pursue whatever was troubling her. Given time, she'd tell him, anyway.

"There's a little restaurant on Fourth. A hole in the wall, but the food's excellent."

"That'll be fine," she said formally.

She knew that his hand at her elbow was meant to guide her. Today it was a stimulation she didn't want or need. It wasn't fair that the only man she'd ever really fallen for preferred women who frequented a sleazy bar — and worse. Remembering the type of people at Soft Sam's, Jayne knew she could never be as worldly and sophisticated as they were. There was no point in even pretending. She wasn't that good an actress.

"You're quiet today." Riley led the way outside to his parked car and in a few minutes pulled into the busy afternoon traffic.

She managed a smile. "I sent in my money for the reunion this morning. It's less than a month away now."

"I'm looking forward to it." Riley studied her, growing more confused by the minute. Whatever was bothering her was more serious than he'd first believed. He forced himself not to pressure her to talk.

"So am I."

"I missed seeing you Saturday evening. You said you had a surprise for me." He found a parking space and pulled into it. "The restaurant's over there. I hope you like Creole cooking."

"That sounds fine."

He noted that she'd avoided responding to his first statement. "I recommend the shrimp-stuffed eggplant."

"That's what I'll order then." It would be a miracle if she could choke down any lunch.

They were seated almost immediately and handed menus. The selection wasn't large, but judging by the spicy smells wafting from the kitchen, Jayne guessed that the food would be as good as Riley claimed.

"I tried to call you Sunday," he told her, setting his menu aside. "I didn't leave a message."

"I rented a car and drove to Seaside for the day."

Riley knitted his brow. She'd left the apartment to get away from him. He would have sworn that was the

reason. "You should've said something. I would have taken you."

Jayne lowered her eyes. "I didn't
want to trouble you."

"It wouldn't have been any trouble.
The trip could have been interesting.
I've heard a lot about the Oregon
coastline, but haven't had the chance
to see it yet."

"It's lovely."

The waitress came, and they placed
their order.

Jayne twisted the paper napkin in
her lap, staring down at it, not looking at him.

"What did you do in Seaside all
day?"

"Walked. And thought." She hadn't
meant to admit that.

"And what were you thinking
about?"

"You." No point in lying. Her eye would twitch, and he'd know, anyway.

"What did you decide?"

"That I wasn't going to let you hurt me," she whispered fervently.

He'd hurt her in the past and had discovered that any pain she suffered mirrored his own at having done something to upset her. "I would never purposely hurt you, Jayne."

He already had. Her napkin was shredded in half. "I'm different from other women you know, Riley. But being . . . inexperienced shouldn't be a fault."

"I consider your lack of experience a virtue." He didn't know where all this was leading, but they were on the right path.

A virtue! Jayne almost laughed. He'd gone from her arms to those of

195

that . . . other woman without so much as a hint of conscience.

Their lunch arrived, and Jayne stared at the large pink shrimp that filled the crispy fried eggplant. She had no appetite.

"Why'd you change your hair?"

Jayne picked up her fork, refusing to meet his probing gaze. "For the reunion."

"Is that the only reason?"

"Should there be another one?"

"You said you had a surprise for me," he coaxed.

"Not exactly *for* you."

"I see." He didn't, but it shouldn't matter.

Tasting a shrimp, Jayne marveled at the wonderful flavors. "This is good."

"I thought you'd enjoy it."

They ate in silence for several minutes. Riley's appetite was quickly satisfied. He'd finished his meal before Jayne was one-third done. He saw the way she toyed with the shrimp, eating only a couple before laying her fork on the plate and pushing it aside.

"I guess I'm not very hungry," she murmured.

Riley crumpled his paper napkin. "Why is it so important for you to go to that reunion?" he asked bluntly.

Jayne had asked herself the same question over and over. Her hand went around the water glass. The condensation on the outside wet her hand, and she wiped her fingers dry on a fresh napkin.

"I'm not sure," she finally said. "I'd like to see everyone again. It's been a long time."

"You've kept in contact with them?"

"A few. Mainly a girl named Judy Thomas. She was the closest friend I had there."

"What about the boys?" They were the ones who worried Riley. Once her male classmates realized what an unspoiled beauty she'd turned out to be, they might give him a run for his money. He wouldn't relinquish this woman easily. He'd waited a lifetime for her.

"There weren't any. I attended a private girls' school."

Riley smiled at the unexpected relief that went through him. "That must have been tough."

"Not really. I attended a women's college, as well."

"So that's where you got your case of repressed relationship development." He tried to make a joke of it but saw quickly that his humor had fallen flat. Riley was baffled at the ready tears that sprang to her eyes.

"Jayne, I didn't mean that the way it sounded." His hand reached for hers.

Jayne jerked her fingers away. "Did you enjoy her, Riley?"

The question was asked in such a small, broken voice that his face tightened with alarm. "Who?"

"The blonde from Soft Sam's."

Six

Regret went through Riley like a hot knife. Little wonder Jayne had been avoiding him. But how could he ever explain this to her? "You saw me?"

"I saw both of you," Jayne whispered. Her soft, pain-filled gaze held his, begging him to tell her it wasn't true. That she was mistaken, and it was only someone who resembled him.

Riley considered lying to her. She might have believed him, but Riley couldn't and wouldn't do it. "I wasn't with her for the reason you think."

Jayne closed her eyes for a moment. "What other reason could there be? I may be inexperienced, but I'm not stupid."

"We're friends." That was a huge exaggeration, but it wouldn't be wise to tell her any more than that for her own safety. Priestly had introduced him to the blonde, and later Riley had used his influence to get her off prostitution charges. By doing so, he'd gotten all the information she could feed him. He couldn't expect Jayne to understand any of this. For that matter, telling her the truth could put her in danger, and he refused to risk that.

"From the look of it, I'd say you were *very* good friends." To her humiliation, Jayne's voice cracked, but she continued speaking in a hoarse whisper. "How could you go to . . . her after the wonderful morning we shared? That's what hurts the most, knowing that you —"

"Jayne, I swear on everything I hold dear that I didn't touch her." His deep voice had a fervency she'd never heard from him.

Jayne desperately wanted to believe Riley, but she didn't know if she dared. He had the potential to hurt her more than anyone. Trusting him now could prove to be a terrible mistake later. "Then why were you with her?"

"I told you. She's a friend." His gaze didn't waver under the scrutiny of hers.

Jayne lowered her eyes to the lunch she'd barely tasted. "What does she have that I don't?"

"Jayne . . ."

"You went from my arms to hers with hardly a breath in between. Tell me. I want to know. What attracted you to this particular *friend* on this particular Saturday?"

Riley hedged. "The arrangements to meet had already been made. I would've met with her even if I hadn't been with you that morning."

"I see."

"I'm sure you don't, and quite honestly, I wouldn't blame you if you didn't believe me. But I'm asking you to trust me." He paused to study her tight features and silently cursed himself for the timing of this relationship. If he was going to fall in love, why did it have to be *now*? He felt torn. There was so much to live for with Jayne in his life. He had to get out of this business, and the quicker the better. For his sake as well as hers.

"I want to trust you." Indecision played across her face.

"Can you believe that I didn't touch her?" he asked.

In response, her eyes delved into his. "I believe you," she murmured. She had to trust Riley or go crazy picturing him in the arms of another woman. The image would destroy her.

"There's only one woman who interests me."

"Oh?"

"One exceptionally lovely woman with honey-brown eyes and a heart so full of love she can't help giving it away." He remembered finding her with the children in the library and again felt such overwhelming desire for her that he ached with it. As he watched her, he could picture her with their child. Until recently, Riley hadn't given much thought to a family. Because of his job, he lived hard, often encountering danger, even when he least expected it. No, that wasn't true; he *always* expected it. He'd seen other men, men with families, attempt to balance their two worlds, and the results could be disastrous. In an effort to avoid that, Riley had pushed any hope of a permanent relationship from his mind, and succeeded. Until he met Jayne.

"Come on," he said, standing. "Let's get out of here." He pulled his wallet from his back pocket and tossed a few bills on the table before waving to someone in the back kitchen. Then he led her outside.

When Jayne moved toward his car, Riley stopped her and directed her to a dark alley.

"I know this isn't the right time or place," he whispered, pressing her against the building's brick wall. His hands were on both sides of her face. "But I need this."

He kissed her hungrily, and Jayne responded the same way.

She couldn't get enough of him. She could feel his kiss in every part of her. Sensations tingled along her nerves. The doubts that had weighed on her mind dissolved and with them the pain of the past two days. Lifting her arms, she slid them around his middle and arched toward him.

"Oh, my sweet Jayne." His voice was raspy and filled with emotion. "Trust me, for just a little longer."

"Forever," she whispered in return. "Forever and ever."

Riley closed his eyes. With his current case he was going to demand a lot more of her trust. He wanted to protect her and himself and walk away from this part of his life and start anew. His prayer was that they could hold on to this moment for all time, but he already knew that was impossible.

When Jayne got back to the library, she was ten minutes late. Her lips were devoid of lipstick and her hair was mussed.

"Sorry I'm late," she said, taking her seat and avoiding Gloria's probing gaze.

"Where'd you go?"

"I . . . don't recall the name of the

restaurant, but they serve Creole food. It's on Fourth."

"They must've been busy."

"Why?" Jayne's eyes flew to her friend.

"Because you're late."

"As a matter of fact, we were lucky to find a table." Her right eye gave one convulsive jerk, and she quickly changed the subject. "Have you heard from Lance?"

"I already told you we're going out again tonight."

"So you did," Jayne mumbled, having momentarily forgotten.

"He's wonderful."

"I'm really happy for you." Who would have believed that after months of searching, Gloria would finally meet someone in the frozen-food section of Albertsons?

"Don't be in too much of a hurry to congratulate me," Gloria said. "It's too soon to tell if he's a keeper. So far, I like him quite a bit, and we seem to have several common interests — besides groceries. But then that's not always good, either."

"Why not?" The more time Jayne spent with Riley, the more she discovered that they enjoyed many of the same things. They were alike and yet completely different.

"Boring."

Jayne blinked. "I beg your pardon?"

Gloria took a chair beside her and crossed her legs. "Sometimes people are so much alike that they end up boring each other to death."

"That won't be a problem with Riley and me. In fact, I was thinking that although we're alike in some ways, we're quite different in others." Smiling, she looked at Gloria. "I like him, you know. I may even love him."

Gloria smiled back. "I know."

"I'm trying a new recipe for spaghetti sauce, if you'd like to come over for dinner," Jayne told Riley on Friday morning. He gave her a ride downtown most days now and phoned whenever he couldn't. His working hours often extended beyond hers, so she still took the bus home in the evenings. But things had worked out well. Since she arrived home first, she started preparing supper, taking pleasure in creating meals because it gave her an excuse to invite Riley over.

"I'll bring the wine."

"Okay." She smiled up at him with

little of her former shyness.

"Jayne —" he paused, taking her hand "— you don't have to lure me to your place with wonderful meals."

Her eyes dropped. She hadn't thought her methods were quite that transparent. "I enjoy cooking," she said lamely.

"I just don't want you going to all this trouble for me. I want to be with you, whether you feed me or not. It's you I'm attracted to. Not your cooking. Well, not *just* your cooking."

"I like being with you, too."

Since their lunch on Monday, they'd spent every available minute in each other's company. Often they didn't do anything more exciting than watch television. One night they'd sat together, each engrossed in a good book, and shared a bottle of excellent white wine. That whole evening they hadn't spoken more than a dozen times. But Jayne had never felt closer to another human being.

Riley kissed her and touched her often. It wasn't uncommon for him to sneak up behind her when she was standing at the stove or rinsing dishes. But he never let their kissing get out of control. Jayne wasn't half as eager to restrain their lovemaking as Riley seemed to be.

That evening Jayne had the sauce simmering on the stove and was ready to add the dry spaghetti to the boiling water when Riley called.

"I'm going to be late," he said gruffly.

"That's fine. I can hold dinner."

"I don't think you should." His

voice tightened. "In fact, maybe you'd better eat without me."

"I don't want to." She'd been having her meals alone almost every night of her adult life, and suddenly the thought held no appeal.

"This can't be helped, Jayne."

The city worked its inspectors harder than necessary, in Jayne's opinion. "I understand." She didn't really, but asking a flurry of questions wouldn't help. As it was, his responses were clipped and impatient.

He sighed into the phone, and Jayne thought she heard a car honk in the background. "I'll talk to you in the morning," he said.

"Sure, the morning will be fine. I'll save some dinner for you, and you can have it for lunch. Spaghetti's always better the next day."

"Great," he said. She heard a loud shout. "I've got to go," he said hurriedly.

"See you tomorrow."

"Right, tomorrow," Riley said with an earnestness that caused a cold chill to race up Jayne's spine. She held on to the phone longer than necessary, her fingers tightening around the receiver. As she hung up, a feeling of dread settled in the pit of her stomach. Riley hadn't been calling her from his office. The sounds in the background were street noises. And he was with someone. A male. Something was wrong. She could feel it. Something was very, very wrong.

Jayne didn't sleep well that night, tossing and turning while her short conversation with Riley played back in her mind. She went over every detail. He'd sounded impatient, angry. His voice was hard and flat, reminding her of the first few times she'd talked to him.

When she finally did drift off to sleep, her dreams were troubled. Visions of Riley with that woman from Soft Sam's drifted into her mind until she woke with an abrupt start. The dream had been so real that goose bumps broke out on her arms, and she hugged her blankets closer.

The following morning, Saturday, Riley was at her door early. Jayne had barely dressed and had just finished her breakfast.

"Morning." She smiled, not quite meeting his gaze.

"Morning." He leaned forward and brushed his mouth over hers. "I'm sorry about last night." He gently pressed his hands against the sides of her neck, forcing her to meet his eyes.

"That's okay. I understand. There are times I need to work late, as well." All her fears seemed trivial now. He was a city inspector, so naturally he didn't spend all his time in an office or on his own. She'd overacted. Her niggling worries about why he'd canceled melted away under the warmth of his gaze.

He broke away from her and walked to the other side of her living room. "This next week is going to be busy, so maybe we shouldn't make any dinner plans."

Jayne rubbed her hands together. "If that's what you want."

"It isn't."

He said it with such honesty that Jayne could find no reason to doubt him.

After a cup of coffee, they left for Riverside Park. Together they did the shopping for the week, making several stops. When they returned to the apartment building, their arms were filled with packages.

"I want to stop off at the manager's," Riley announced as they stepped into the elevator.

"I'll go on up to my place and put these things away." She didn't want the ice cream to melt while Riley paid his rent.

"I'll be up shortly."

The elevator doors closed, and Jayne watched the light that indicated the floor numbers. She smiled at Riley, recalling similar rides in times past and how she'd dreaded being caught alone with him. Now she savored the moment.

Riley smiled back. Their morning had been marvelous, he thought. It seemed natural to have Jayne at his side, and he'd enjoyed going shopping together like a long-married couple. He experienced a surge of tenderness that was so powerful it was akin to pain. He'd been waiting for this woman for years. He was deeply grateful to have her in his life, especially after the unsavory people he'd been dealing with these past few years. He loved her wry wit. Her sense of humor was subtle and quick. Thinking about it now made him chuckle lightly.

"Is something funny?" She raised wide inquisitive eyes to him.

"No, just thinking about you."

"I'm so glad I amuse you." She

shifted her shopping bag from one hand to the other.

"Here." Deliberately he took her bag and set it on the elevator floor. Before she could realize what he was doing, he turned her in his embrace and slid his arms around her waist. "You're the most beautiful woman I've ever met, Jayne Gilbert."

"Oh, Riley." She lowered her gaze, not knowing how to respond. No man had ever said anything so wonderful to her. From someone else it would have sounded like a well-worn line, but she could see the sincerity in his eyes. That told her *he* believed it, even if she couldn't.

"Do you doubt me?"

She answered him with a short nod. "I've seen myself in plenty of mirrors. I know what I look like."

"An angel. Pure, good, innocent." With each word, he drew closer to her. Sweeping her hair aside, he brushed her neck with his mouth. She tilted her head, and the brown curls fell to one side. When his lips moved up her jawline, Jayne felt her legs grow weak. She leaned against the back of the elevator for support. Finally his mouth found hers in a long, slow kiss that left her weak and clinging to him.

The elevator stopped then, and Riley released her for a few seconds, closing the door again.

"Riley, that was our floor," she objected.

"I know." His eyes blazed into hers, and he leaned forward and kissed her again.

Jayne clung to him, awed that this

man could be attracted to her. "I can't believe this," she murmured, and tears clogged her throat.

"What? That we're kissing in an elevator?"

"No," she breathed. "That you're holding me like this. I know it's silly, but I'm afraid of waking up and discovering that this is all a dream. It's too good to be true."

"You'd have a hard time convincing me that this isn't real. You feel too right in my arms."

"You do, too."

Her heart swelled with love. Riley hadn't said he loved her, but he didn't need to. With every action he took and every word he spoke, he was constantly showing her his feelings. For that matter, she hadn't told him how she felt, either. It was unnecessary.

Reluctantly he let her go and pushed the button that would open the elevator doors. "I'll be back in a couple of minutes." He grinned. "I need to go all the way down again."

"I'll start the spaghetti."

"Okay." He caressed her cheek. "I'll see you soon."

She stepped out of the elevator and instantly caught sight of a tall man. She didn't recognize him as anyone from her building and certainly not from the ninth floor. Judging by his age, as well as the leather he wore, he could have been a member of some gang. Jayne swallowed uncomfortably and glanced back at Riley. The elevator doors were closing, and she doubted he saw her panicked look.

Squaring her shoulders, Jayne secured her small purse under her arm and moved the shopping bag to her left hand. Remembering a book she'd read about self-defense, she paused to remove her keys from her purse and held the one for her apartment between her index and middle fingers. If this creep tried to attack she'd be ready. Watching him, Jayne walked to her apartment, which was in the middle of the long corridor. Her breath felt tight in her lungs. With every step she took, the young man advanced toward her.

His eyes were dark, his pupils wide. Fear coated the inside of her mouth. Whoever this was appeared to be high on some sort of drug. All the headlines she'd read about drug-crazed criminals flashed through her mind. Getting into her apartment no longer seemed the safest alternative. What if he forced his way in?

Jayne whirled around and hurried back to the elevator, urgently pushing the button.

"You aren't going to run away, are you?" The man's words were slurred.

In a panic, Jayne pushed the button again. Nothing.

He was so close now that all he had to do was reach out and touch her. Lifting one hand, he pulled her hair and laughed when she winced at the slight pain.

"What do you want?" she demanded, backing away.

"Give me your money."

Jayne had no intention of arguing with him and held out her purse. "I don't have much." Almost all the cash she carried with her had been spent on groceries, and she hadn't brought any credit cards. Or her cell phone . . .

He grabbed her purse and started pawing through it. When he discovered the truth of her statement, he'd be furious, and there was no telling what he'd do next. If she was going to escape, her chance was now.

Raising the bag of groceries, she shoved it into his chest with all her strength and took off running. The stairwell was at the other end of the corridor, and she sprinted toward it. Fear and adrenaline pumped through her, but she wasn't fast enough to beat the young man. He got to the door before she did and blocked her only exit.

Jayne came to an abrupt halt and, with her hands at her sides, moved slowly backward.

She heard the elevator door opening behind her and swung around. Riley stepped out. Jayne's relief was so great she felt like weeping. "Riley!" she called out.

Instantly her attacker straightened.

Riley saw the fear sketched so vividly on her face and felt an overwhelming instinct to protect. Wordlessly he moved toward her pursuer.

The man took one step toward Riley. "Give me your money."

Riley didn't say a word.

In her gratitude at seeing Riley, Jayne hadn't stopped to notice the lack of fear in him. With her back against the wall, her legs gave out, and she slumped helplessly against it.

Riley's face was as hard as granite and so intense that Jayne's breath caught in her lungs. The man who'd kissed her and held her in the elevator wasn't the same man who stood in the hallway now. This Riley was a stranger.

"Hey, buddy, it was just a joke," the young man said, reaching for the doorknob.

Jayne had never seen a man as fierce as Riley was at that moment. She hardly recognized him. Deadly fury blazed from his eyes, and Jayne felt cold shivers racing over her arms.

From there, everything seemed to happen in slow motion. Riley advanced on the young man and knocked him to the ground with one powerful punch.

The man let out a yelp of pain. Riley raised his fist to hit him again. Hand connected with jaw in a sickening thud.

Jayne screamed. "Riley! No more. No more."

As if he'd forgotten she was there, Riley turned back to her. Taking this unexpected opportunity to escape, the man propelled himself through the stairwell door and was gone.

Jayne forced back a tiny sobbing breath and stumbled to his side. She threw her arms around him as tears rained from her eyes. "Oh, Riley," she cried weakly.

Riley's body was rigid against hers for several minutes until the tension eased from his limbs and he wrapped his arms around her. "Did he hurt you?"

"No," she sobbed. "No. He was after my money, but I didn't have much."

His arms went around her with crushing force, driving the air from her lungs.

"If he'd hurt you —"

"He didn't, he didn't." No more words could make it past the constriction in her throat. Jayne realized it wasn't fear that had prompted this sudden paralysis, but the knowledge that Riley was capable of such violence. She didn't want to know what he might've done if she hadn't stopped him.

His hold gradually relaxed. "Tell me what happened," he said, leading her toward her apartment door.

"He wanted my money."

"You didn't do anything stupid like argue with him, did you?"

"No . . . I read in this self-defense book that —"

"You and your books."

She could almost laugh, but not quite. "I'm so grateful you got here when you did." She was thinking of her own safety, but also of the would-be mugger and what Riley would have done to him had he actually hurt her.

"I've never seen anyone fight like that," she murmured, stooping to pick up her purse and the groceries that littered the hallway.

"It's something I learned when I was in the military." Riley strove to make light of what he'd done. The last thing he wanted to do now was to fabricate stories to appease Jayne's curiosity.

He bent down to gather up some of the spilled groceries. Her hands trembled as she deposited one item after another in her bag.

"Are you sure you're all right?" Doubt echoed in his husky voice.

"Yes. I was more scared than anything."

"I don't blame you."

Her returning smile was wooden. "I surprised myself by how quickly I could move."

Getting to his feet, Riley brought the bag with him. "Let's get these things put away. I'll bet the ice cream is starting to melt."

Rushing ahead of him to unlock the apartment door, Jayne had the freezer open by the time he arrived in her kitchen. He handed the carton of vanilla ice cream to her; she shoved it inside and closed the door.

"Do you think we should call the police?" she asked, still shaking.

"No. He won't be back."

"How do you know?" His confidence was unnerving.

"I just do. But if it'll make you feel better, go ahead and call them."

"I might." She watched for his reaction, but he gave none. Maybe it was her imagination, but she had the distinct feeling that Riley didn't want her to contact the authorities.

Riley paced the floor. "Jayne, listen, I've got something to tell you."

"Yes?" She raised expectant eyes to him.

"I'm going away for a while."

"Away?"

"On vacation. A fishing trip. I'm leaving tonight."

SEVEN

"A fishing trip?" Jayne asked incredulously. Riley didn't know the difference between a salmon and a trout. "Isn't this rather sudden?"

"Not really. The timing looked good, so we decided to go now, instead of waiting until later in the summer." Riley opened the refrigerator and took out the bowl of spaghetti sauce, setting it on the counter.

Jayne moved to the cupboard and got a saucepan. She worked for the city, too, and knew from experience that vacation times were often planned a year in advance. One didn't simply decide "the timing looked good" and head off on vacation. "How long will you be gone?"

His eyes softened. "Don't worry. I'll be back in time for your reunion."

Jayne was apprehensive, but it wasn't over her high school reunion. This so-called vacation of Riley's had a fishy odor that had nothing to do with trout. Busy at the sink, she kept her back to him, swallowing down her doubts. "You must have had this planned for quite a while."

"Not really. It was a spur-of-the-moment decision." He didn't elaborate, and she didn't ask. Quizzing him about the particulars would only put a strain on these last few hours together.

She *should* ask him about these

spur-of-the-moment vacation plans and how he'd arranged it with the city. From what he'd told her, Riley was a city inspector. But Jayne had doubts about that; she couldn't help it. Although he seemed to keep regular hours, he often needed to meet someone at night. She'd watched him several times from her living room window, seeing him in the parking lot below. She'd never questioned him about his late hours, though, afraid of what she'd discover if she pursued the subject.

She bit her bottom lip, angry with herself for being so complacent.

"You've got that look on your face," Riley said when she set the pan of water on the stove to boil.

"What look?"

"The one that tells me you disapprove."

"How could I possibly object to you taking a well-deserved vacation? You've been working long hours. You need a break. Right?"

"Right."

But he didn't sound as though he was excited about this trip. And from little things he'd let drop, Jayne suspected he didn't even know what a fishing pole looked like. He certainly didn't know anything about fish!

Standing behind her, Riley slipped his arms around her waist and pressed his mouth to the side of her neck. "A watched pot never boils," he murmured. "Jayne, listen — I shouldn't be gone any more than ten days. Two weeks at the most."

"Two weeks!" The reunion was in

three. Turning, she hugged him with all the pent-up love in her heart. "I'll miss you," she whispered.

"I'll miss you, too." Tenderly, he kissed her temple, then tilted her head so that his mouth could claim hers.

Jayne marveled that he could be so loving and gentle only minutes after punching out a mugger. The whole incident had frightened her. There were depths to this man that she had yet to glimpse, dangerous depths. But perhaps it was better not to see that side of his nature. An icy sensation ran down her arms, and she shivered.

"You're cold."

"No," she said. "Afraid."

"Why?" He tightened his hold. "What do you have to fear?"

"I don't know."

"That mugger won't be back."

"I know." After what Riley had done to him, Jayne was confident the man wouldn't dare return.

Forcing down her apprehension, she smiled and raised her fingers to his thick dark hair, then arched up and kissed his mouth. She was being unnecessarily silly, she told herself. Riley was going on a fishing trip. He'd return before her reunion, and everything would be wonderful again.

Reluctantly breaking away from him, she sighed. "I'll get lunch started. You probably have a hundred things you need to do this afternoon."

"What things?"

"What about getting all your gear together?" She added the dry noodles to the rapidly boiling water, wanting to believe with all her heart that Riley was doing exactly as he'd said.

"The other guy is bringing everything."

"But surely you've got stuff you need to do."

"Perhaps, but I decided I'd rather spend the day with you."

"When are you leaving?" One of her uncles was an avid sportsman, and from what Jayne remembered, he was emphatic that early morning was the best time for fishing.

"Tonight."

"Where will you be? Are you camping?"

He shrugged. "I don't know. I've left all the arrangements to my friend."

That sounded highly questionable, and her manufactured confidence quickly crumpled. Under the weight of her uncertainty, Jayne bowed her head.

"Honey." He tucked a finger beneath her chin, and her eyes lifted to his. "I'll be back in no time."

Despite her fears, Jayne laughed. "I sincerely doubt that." He hadn't even gone, and she already felt an empty void in her life.

"I know how important your reunion is to you."

Riley was more important to her than a hundred high school reunions. A thought went crashing through her mind with such searing impact that for a moment she was stunned. She wondered if she'd finally figured out why Riley paid her so much attention. "You seem awfully worried about my reunion."

"Only because I know how much

you want to go."

With trembling hands she brought down two dinner plates from the cupboard. "I don't need your charity or your pity, Riley Chambers."

"What are you talking about?" His jaw sagged open in astonished disbelief.

Jayne's brown eyes burned with the fiery light of outrage. "It just dawned on me that . . . that all this attention you've been giving me lately could be attributed to precisely those reasons."

"Charity?" he demanded. "Pity? You don't honestly believe that!"

"I don't know what to think anymore. Why else would someone as . . . as worldly as you have anything to do with someone as plain and ordinary as me?"

Riley stared at her in shock. Jayne, plain and ordinary! Vivacious and outgoing she wasn't. But Jayne was special — more than any woman he'd ever known. He opened his mouth to speak, closed it and stalked across the room. What had gotten into her? He'd never known Jayne to be illogical. From her reaction, he could tell she wasn't falling for this fishing story of his. Telling her had been difficult enough. He hadn't wanted to do it, but there was no other option. He couldn't tell her the real reason for this unexpected "vacation," but he was lying to her for her own protection. The fewer people who were in on it, the better.

Jayne carried the plates to the table, feeling angry, hurt and confused; most of all, she was suspicious. How easily she'd been swayed by his charm and his kisses. She'd been a pushover for a man of Riley's experience. From the beginning she'd known that he wasn't everything he appeared to be. But she'd preferred to overlook the obvious. Riley was up to no good. She told herself she had a right to know what he was doing, and yet in the same breath, she had no desire to venture into the unknown mysteries he'd been hiding from her.

"Jayne, please look at me," he said quietly. "You can't accuse me of something as ridiculous as pitying you, then walk away."

"I didn't walk away . . . I'm setting the table." She turned to face him, her expression defiant.

"Charity, Jayne? Pity? I think you

need to explain yourself."

"What's there to explain? I've always been a joke to people like you. Except that for a woman who's supposed to be smart, I've been incredibly stupid."

Riley was at a complete loss. His past dealings with women had been brief. In his line of work, it had been preferable to avoid any emotional ties. Now he discovered that he didn't know how to reassure Jayne, the first woman who'd touched his heart. He couldn't be entirely honest, but perhaps a bit of logic wouldn't be amiss. . . .

"Even if you're right and everything I feel for you is of a charitable nature," he began, "what's my motive?"

"I don't know. But then I wouldn't, would I?"

He took a step toward her and paused. He couldn't rush her, although every instinct urged him to take her in his arms and comfort her. "That's not what's really bothering you, is it?"

Tears clouded her eyes as she shook her head. "No."

He reached for her, but Jayne avoided him. "Honey . . ." he murmured.

She blanched and pointed a shaking finger in his direction. "Don't call me *honey*. I'm not important to you."

"I love you, Jayne." He didn't know any other way to tell her. The flowery words she deserved and probably expected just weren't in him. He could only hope she trusted him — and that she'd give him time.

Jayne's reaction was to place her

hand over her mouth and shake her head from side to side.

"Well?" he said impatiently. "Don't you have anything to say?"

Jayne stared at him, her eyes wet. "You *love* me?"

"It can't have been any big secret. You must've known, for heaven's sake."

"Riley . . ."

"No, it's your turn to listen. I've gone about this all wrong. Women like moonlight, roses, the whole deal." He paced the kitchen and ran a hand through his hair. "I'm no good at this. With you, I wanted to do everything right, and already I can see it's backfiring."

"Riley, I love you, too."

"Women need romance. I realize that and I feel like a jerk because you're entitled to all of it. Unfortunately, I don't know the right words to tell you about everything inside me."

"Riley." She said his name again, her voice gaining volume. "Did you hear what I said?"

"I know you love me," he muttered almost angrily. "You aren't exactly one to disguise your feelings."

She crossed her arms over her chest with an exasperated sigh. "Well, excuse me."

"I'm not good enough for you," he continued, barely acknowledging her response. "Someone as honorable and kind as you deserves a man who's a heck of a lot better than me. I've lived hard these past few years and I've done more than one thing I regret."

Jayne started to respond but wasn't given the opportunity.

"There hasn't been room in my life for a woman. But I can't wait any longer. I didn't realize how much I need you. I want to change, but that's going to take time and patience."

"I'm patient," Jayne told him shyly, her anger forgotten under the sweet balm of his words. "Gloria says I'm the most patient person she's ever known. In fact, my father gets angry with me because he feels I'm too meek . . . not that meekness and patience are the same thing, you understand. It's just that —"

"Are you going to chatter all day, or are you going to come over here and let me kiss you?" His eyes took on a fierce possessive light.

"Oh, Riley, I love you so much."

She walked into his waiting arms, surrendering everything — her heart, her soul, her life. And her doubts.

They kissed, lightly at first, testing their freshly revealed emotions. Then their lips stayed together, gradually parting as their mouths moved, slanting, tasting, probing.

Jayne whimpered. She couldn't help herself. There was so much more she longed to discover. . . .

His kisses deepened until he raised his head and whispered hoarsely. "Jayne. Oh, my sweet, sweet, Jayne."

"I love you," she said again and kissed him softly.

Riley tunneled his fingers through her hair and buried his face in the slope of her neck. But he didn't push her away as he had in the past. Nor did he bring her closer. His breath was rushed as he struggled with indecision.

"Riley . . ."

"Shhh, don't move. Okay?"

"Okay," she agreed, loving him more and more.

Gradually the tension eased from him, and he relaxed. But his hold didn't loosen, and he held her for what seemed like hours rather than minutes.

They spent the rest of the day together. After lunch they walked in the park, holding hands, making excuses to touch each other. Riley brought along a chessboard and set it up on the picnic table, and they played a long involved game. When Jayne won the match, Riley applauded her skill and reset the board. He won the second game. They decided against a third.

At dinnertime they ate Chinese food at a small hole-in-the-wall restaurant and brought the leftovers home.

Standing just inside her apartment door, Jayne asked, "Do you want to come in for coffee?"

"I've got to pack and get ready."

She nodded. "I understand. Thank you for today."

"No, thank *you.*" He laid his hand against her cheek, and when he spoke, his voice was warm and filled with emotion. "You'll take care of yourself while I'm gone, won't you?"

"Of course I will." She couldn't resist smiling. "I've been doing a fairly good job of that for several years now."

"I don't feel right leaving you." He

studied her. He wished this case was over so he could give her all the things she had a right to ask for.

"You're coming back."

The words stung his conscience. There was always the possibility that he wouldn't. The risks and dangers of his job had been a stimulant before he'd fallen in love with Jayne. Now he experienced the first real taste of dread.

Fear shot through Jayne at the expression on Riley's face. She saw the way his eyes narrowed, the way his mouth tightened. "You *are* coming back, aren't you?" She repeated her question, louder and stronger this time.

"I'll be back." His voice vibrated with emotion. "I love you, Jayne. I'm coming back to you, don't worry."

Not worry! One glimpse at the intense look in his eyes, and she was terrified. From the way Riley was behaving, one would assume that he was going off on a suicide mission.

Riley smiled and brought his hand to her face. He touched her cheek, then her forehead, easing the frown between her brows. "I'll be back. I promise you that."

"I'll be waiting."

"I won't be able to contact you."

She nodded.

The story about his fishing trip was forgotten. Jayne didn't know where he was headed or why. For now, she didn't want to know. He said he was coming back, and that was all that mattered.

"Goodbye, my love," he said with a final kiss.

"Goodbye, Riley."

He turned and walked out the door, and Jayne was left with an aching void of uncertainty.

The library was busy on Monday morning. Jayne was sitting at the information desk in the children's department when the chief librarian approached, carrying a huge bouquet of red roses in a lovely ceramic vase.

"How beautiful," Jayne said, looking up.

"They just arrived for you." Her boss placed them on the desk.

"For me?" No one had ever sent her flowers at work.

Gloria walked across the room and joined her. "Who are they from?" she asked, then answered her own question. "It must be Riley."

"Must be." Jayne unpinned the small card and pulled it from the envelope.

"What's it say?" Gloria wanted to know.

"Just that he'll be home by the time these wilt."

"He must have sent them from out of town."

Jayne frowned. "Right." Except that the card was scrawled in Riley's own unmistakable handwriting. He could have ordered them before he went, or . . . or maybe he hadn't left Portland yet.

She squelched the doubts and possibilities that raced through her mind. She loved Riley and he loved her, and that was all that mattered. Not where he was or what he was doing. Or even whether he was fishing.

Without him, the days passed slowly. Jayne was astonished that a man she'd known and loved for such a short time could so effectively fill her life. Now her days lacked purpose. She went to work, came home and plopped down in front of the television. During the first week that he was gone, Jayne ate more microwave dinners than she'd eaten the whole previous month. It was simpler that way.

"You look like you could do with some cheering up," Gloria commented Friday afternoon.

"I could," Jayne murmured.

"How about if we go shopping tomorrow for a dress to wear to your reunion? I know just the place."

Jayne would need something special for the reunion, but she didn't feel like shopping. Still, it had to be done sooner or later. "All right," she found herself agreeing.

"And in exchange for my expert advice, you can take me to the Creole restaurant where you and Riley had lunch."

"Sure. If I can remember where it is. We only went there once." That day had been so miserable for Jayne that she hadn't paid much attention to the place or the food.

"You said it was on Fourth."

"Right." She remembered now, and she also recalled why she'd been so miserable. That was when she'd seen Riley with the blonde.

Gloria showed up at her apartment early Saturday morning. Jayne had no enthusiasm for this shopping expedition.

Gloria got a carton of orange juice from the refrigerator and poured herself a glass. "I checked out this new boutique, and it's expensive, but worth it."

"Gloria." Jayne sighed. The longer Riley was away, the more unsure she felt about the reunion. "I've probably got something adequate in my closet."

"You don't." Gloria opened the fridge again and peeked inside. "I'm starved. Have you had breakfast yet?"

Jayne hadn't. "I'm not hungry, but help yourself."

"Thanks." Pulling out a loaf of bread, Gloria stuck a piece in the toaster. "When you walk in the grand ballroom of the Seattle Westin, I want every eye to be on you."

"I'll see what I can do to arrange a spotlight," Jayne said.

"I mean it. You're going to be a hit."

"Right." In twenty-seven years, she hadn't made an impression on anything except her mattress.

"Hey, where's your confidence? You can't back down now. You've got the man, kiddo. It's all downhill from here."

"I suppose," Jayne said.

"I thought you should get something in red."

"Red?" Jayne echoed with a small laugh. "I was thinking more along the lines of brown or beige."

"Nope." The toast popped up, and Gloria buttered it. "You want to stand out in the crowd, not blend in."

"Blending in is what I do."

"Nope." Gloria shook her head.

"For one night, m'dear, you're going to be a knockout."

"Gloria." Jayne hesitated. "I don't know."

"Trust me. I've gotten you this far."

"But . . ."

"Trust me."

Two hours later, Jayne was pleased that she'd had faith in her friend's judgment. After seeing the inside of more stores than she'd visited in a year, she found the perfect dress. Or rather, Gloria did — and not in the new boutique she'd been so excited about, either. This was a classic women's wear shop Jayne would never have ventured into on her own. The dress was a lavender color, and Gloria insisted Jayne try it on. At first, Jayne had scoffed; in two hours, she'd dressed and undressed at least twenty times. She was about to throw up her arms and surrender — nothing fit right, or if it did fit, the color was wrong. Even Gloria showed signs of frustration.

Everything about this full-length gown was perfect. Jayne stood in front of the three-way mirror and blinked in disbelief.

"You look stunning," Gloria breathed in awe.

Jayne couldn't stop staring at herself. This one gown made up for every prom she'd ever missed. The off-the-shoulder style and close-fitting bodice accentuated her full breasts and tiny waist to exquisite advantage. The full side-shirred skirt and double lace ruffle danced about her feet. She couldn't have hoped to find a dress more beautiful.

"Do we dare look at the price?" Gloria murmured, searching for the tag.

"It's lovely, but can I afford it?" Jayne hesitated, expecting to discover some reason she couldn't have this perfect gown.

"You can't afford not to buy it," Gloria stated emphatically. "This is *the* dress for you. Besides, it's a lot more reasonable than I figured." She read the price to her, and Jayne couldn't believe it was so low; she'd assumed it would be twice as much.

"You're buying it, aren't you?" The look Gloria gave her said that if Jayne didn't, she'd never speak to her again.

"Naturally I'm buying it," Jayne responded with a wide grin. Excitement flowed through her, and she felt like singing and dancing. Riley would love how she looked in this dress. Everything was working out so well. She'd shock her former classmates. They'd take one look at her in that gown with Riley at her side, and their jaws would fall open with utter astonishment. And yet . . . that didn't matter the way it once did.

"Now are you going to feed me?" Gloria fluttered her long lashes dramatically as though to say she was about to faint from hunger.

"Do you still want to try that place Riley took me to?"

"Only if we can get there quickly."

Smiling at her friend's humor, Jayne paid for the dress and made arrangements to have it delivered to her apartment later in the day.

She and Gloria chatted easily as they walked out to the street. Gloria drove, and with Jayne acting as navigator, they made their way down the freeway and across the Willamette River to the heart of downtown.

"There it is," Jayne announced as Gloria pulled onto Fourth Avenue. "To your left, about halfway down the block."

"Great." Gloria backed into a parking space. A flash of black attracted Jayne's attention. She glanced into the alley beside the restaurant and saw a sports car similar to Riley's. She immediately decided it wasn't his. There was no reason he'd be here — was there?

"I don't mind telling you I'm starved," Gloria said as she turned off the ignition.

"What's with you lately? I've never known you to show such an interest in food."

"Yes, well, you see . . ." Gloria paused to clear her throat. "I tend to eat when something's bothering me."

"What's bothering you?" Jayne instantly felt guilty. She'd been so involved with her own problems that she hadn't noticed her friend's.

"Well . . ."

"Is it Lance?" It had to be. Gloria hadn't talked about him all week, although the week before she'd been bubbling over about her newfound soul mate. "He's not turning out to be everything you thought?"

"I wish." Gloria reached for her purse and stepped out of the car door.

"What do you wish?"

"That he wasn't so wonderful. Jayne, I'm scared. Look at me." She held out her hand and purposely shook it. "I'm shaking all over."

"But if you like him so much, what's wrong?"

They crossed the street together and entered the restaurant, taking the first available booth. "I've been married once," Gloria told her unnecessarily. "And when that didn't work out, I was sure I'd never recover. I know it sounds melodramatic to anyone who hasn't been through a divorce, but it's true."

Gloria was right; Jayne probably couldn't fully understand, but she thought about Riley and how devastated she'd be if they ever stopped loving each other.

"Now I'm falling for another man and, Jayne, I'm so tied up in knots I can't think straight. Being with you today is an excuse not to be with Lance. Every time we're together, the attraction grows stronger and stronger. We're already talking about marriage."

"I guess it works that way sometimes," Jayne murmured, thinking she'd marry Riley in a minute. Gloria had met Lance only a couple of weeks after Jayne had started seeing Riley.

"We both want a family and we believe strongly in the same things."

"Are you going to marry him?"

Gloria shrugged. "Not yet. It's too serious a decision to make so quickly. Remember the old saying? Marry in haste and repent at leisure."

"And . . ."

"And I haven't told Lance. I know him, or at least I think I know him.

He's just like a man."

"I should hope so." Jayne chuckled.

"Once he decides on something, he wants it *now*. I have this horrible feeling that I'm going to tell him I want to wait, and he's going to argue with me and wear me down. He may even tell me to take a hike. There aren't many men around as good as Lance. I could be walking away from the last opportunity I have to meet a decent man."

"If he loves you, he'll agree. And if he's too impatient, you'll have your answer, won't you?"

"No, because knowing me, I'll want him even more."

The waitress came with glasses of water and a menu. They ordered, ate lunch and chatted over several cups of coffee and cheesecake.

Glancing at her watch, Gloria said, "Listen, I've got to get back. Lance is picking me up in an hour."

Drinking the last of her coffee, Jayne stood. "Then let's get going."

Outside the restaurant, Jayne idly checked the alley for the black car as she crossed the street. It was still there. She could have sworn it was Riley's. But it couldn't be. Could it?

EIGHT

There had to be a thousand black sports cars in Oregon like the one Riley drove, Jayne told herself repeatedly over the next twenty-four hours. Probably more than a thousand. She was being absurd in even wondering if Riley's car was the one in the alley beside the Creole restaurant. He was fishing with friends. Right?

Wrong, said a little voice in the back of her mind. He'd lied about that; Jayne was sure of it. He'd never introduced her to any of his friends. He was new in Portland, having lived in the city for only a few months. He'd admitted there were things in his life he regretted. He'd said he wanted to change and that he wasn't good enough for her.

All weekend, Jayne's thoughts vacillated. Even if he'd lied about the fishing trip, it didn't automatically mean he was doing anything illegal, although those mysterious meetings in the parking lot weren't encouraging. And if he was doing something underhanded, she didn't want to know about it. Ignorance truly was bliss. If she inadvertently found anything out . . . She simply preferred not to know because then she might be required to act on it.

Monday morning on the bus ride into town, Jayne sat looking out the window, the newspaper resting in her

271

lap. She hadn't heard anything from Riley, but then she hadn't expected to.

She glanced at the headlines. The state senator whom she'd met several months earlier had been arrested and released on a large bail. Apparently Senator Max Priestly, who'd lobbied heavily for legalized gambling in Oregon, had ties to the Mafia. She skimmed the article, not particularly interested in the details. His court date had already been set. Jayne felt a grimace of distaste at the thought that a public official would willingly sell out the welfare of his state.

Setting aside the front-page section, she turned to the advice column. Maybe reading about someone else's troubles would lighten her own. It didn't.

At lunchtime Jayne decided not to fight her uncertainty any longer. She'd take a cab to the Creole restaurant and satisfy her curiosity. The black sports car would be gone, and she'd be reassured, calling herself a fool for being so suspicious.

Only she wasn't reassured. Even when she discovered that the car was nowhere to be seen, she didn't relax. Instead she instructed the driver to take her to Soft Sam's.

The minute she climbed out of the taxi, Jayne saw the familiar black car parked on a nearby side street. Her heart pounded against her ribs as dread crept up her spine. Absently she handed the driver his fare.

Just because the car was there didn't mean anything, she told herself calmly. It might not even be his.

But Jayne took one glance at the interior, with Riley's raincoat slung over the seat, and realized it *was* his car.

Stomach churning, Jayne ran her hand over the back fender, confused and unsure. From the beginning of this so-called fishing trip, she'd suspected Riley was lying. She didn't know what he was hiding from her or why — she just knew he was.

Her appetite gone, Jayne backed away from the car and returned to the library without eating lunch.

That evening when she arrived at her apartment, Jayne turned on the TV to drown out her fears. The first time she'd ever seen Riley, she'd thought he looked like . . . well, like a criminal. Some underworld gang member. He wore that silly raincoat as if he were carrying something he wanted to conceal — like a gun.

Slumping onto the sofa, Jayne buried her face in her hands. *Could* he be hiding a weapon? The very idea was ridiculous. Of course he wasn't! She'd know if he carried a gun. He'd held her enough for her to have felt it.

The local news blared from the TV. The evening broadcast featured the arrest of Senator Max Priestly, who'd been caught in a sting operation. This was the same story she'd read in the morning paper.

Jayne stared at the screen and at the outrage that showed on Priestly's face. He shouted that he'd been framed and he'd prove his innocence in court. The commentator came back to say that the state's case had been damaged by the mysterious disappearance of vital evidence.

Deciding she'd had enough unsavory news, Jayne stood and turned off the TV.

In bed that night, she kept changing positions. Nothing felt comfortable. She couldn't vanquish her niggling doubts, couldn't relax. When she did drift into a light sleep, her dreams were filled with Riley and Senator Max Priestly. Waking in a cold sweat, Jayne lay staring at the dark ceiling, wondering why her mind had connected the two men.

Pounding her pillow, she rolled onto her side and forced her eyes to close. A burning sensation went through her, and her eyes opened with sudden alarm. She'd connected the two men because she'd seen Riley *with*

Max Priestly. She hadn't met the state senator at the library, as she'd assumed. She'd seen him with Riley. But when? Weeks ago, she recalled, before she'd started dating Riley. Where? Closing her eyes again, she tried to drag up the details of the meeting. It must have been at the apartment. Yes, he was the man in the parking lot. She'd seen Priestly hand Riley a briefcase. At the time, Jayne remembered that Senator Priestly had looked vaguely familiar. Later, she'd associated him with the group of state legislators that had toured the library. But Max Priestly hadn't been one of them.

And Riley wasn't on any fishing trip. If he was somehow linked with this man — and he appeared to be — then he probably knew that

Priestly had been arrested. Riley could very well have spent this "vacation" of his awaiting Priestly's bail hearing. No wonder he hadn't been able to give her the exact date of his return.

The first thing Jayne did the next morning was to rip through the paper, eagerly searching for more information. She didn't need to look far. Again Max Priestly dominated the front page. An interview with his secretary reported that the important missing evidence was telephone logs and copies of letters Max had dictated to her. They'd simply disappeared from her computer. When questioned about how long they'd been missing, the secretary claimed that their absence had been discovered only recently. After that, Jayne stopped reading.

The morning passed in a fog of regret. Jayne didn't know what her coworkers must think of her. She felt like a robot, programmed to act and do certain assignments without thought or question, and that was what she'd done.

When Gloria started talking about her relationship with Lance during their coffee break, Jayne didn't hear a word. She nodded and smiled at the appropriate times and prayed her friend wouldn't notice.

"Isn't it terrible, all this stuff that's coming out about Senator Priestly?"

Jayne's coffee sloshed over the rim of her cup. "Yes," she mumbled, avoiding Gloria's eyes.

"The news this morning said he has connections to the underworld. Apparently he was hoping to promote prostitution rings along with legalized gambling."

"Prostitution," Jayne echoed, vividly recalling the bleached blonde on Riley's arm that afternoon. She'd refused to believe he had anything to do with the woman, even though she knew what the woman was. Somehow she'd even managed to overcome the pain of seeing Riley with her. Now she realized that Soft Sam's was more than simply a bar. Riley had repeatedly warned her to stay away from it. She hadn't needed his caution; Jayne had felt so out of place during her one visit that she wouldn't have returned under any circumstances.

After her coffee break with Gloria, Jayne's day went from bad to worse. Nothing seemed to go right for the rest of the afternoon.

That evening, stepping off the bus, she saw Riley's car parked in his spot across the street. He was back. A chill went through her. She wouldn't tell him what she knew but prayed that he loved her enough to be honest with her.

She hadn't been inside the apartment for more than five minutes when Riley was at her door. Jayne froze at the sound of his knock. Squaring her shoulders, she forced a smile on her lips.

"Welcome back," she said, pulling open the door.

Riley took one look at her pale features and walked into the apartment. For nearly two weeks, he'd tried to put Jayne out of his mind and concentrate on his assignment. A mistake could have been disastrous, even deadly. Yet he hadn't been able to forget her. She'd been with him every minute. All he'd needed to do was close his eyes and she'd be there. Her image, her memory, comforted him and brought him joy. *So this was love.* He'd avoided it for years, but now he realized the way he felt was beyond description.

"I've missed you," he whispered, reaching for her.

Willingly Jayne went into his arms. She couldn't doubt the sincerity in his low voice.

"Oh, Riley." His name became an aching sigh as she wound her arms around his neck and buried her face in his chest.

Her tense muscles immediately communicated to Riley that something was wrong. "Honey," he breathed into her hair. "What is it?" His hand curved around the side of her neck, his fingers tangling with her soft curls. He raised her head the fraction of an inch needed for her lips to meet his descending mouth. He'd dreamed of kissing her for days. . . .

Jayne moaned softly. She loved this man. It didn't matter what he'd done or who he knew. Riley had said he wanted to change. Jayne's love would be the bridge that would link him to a clean, honest life. Together they'd work to undo any wrong Riley had been involved in before he met her. She'd help him. She'd do nothing, absolutely nothing, to destroy this blissful happiness they shared.

Their gentle exploratory kiss grew more intense. Riley lifted his head.

"Oh, my love," he moaned raggedly into the hollow of her throat. "I've missed you so much."

"I missed you, too," she whispered in return.

He buried his hands deep in her hair and didn't breathe. Then he mumbled something she couldn't hear and reluctantly broke the contact.

For days he'd dreamed about the feel of her in his arms, yet his imagination fell short of reality. Her lips were warm and swollen from his kisses, and he could hardly believe that this shy, gentle woman could raise such havoc with his senses. "Has anything interesting happened around here?" he asked, trying to distract himself.

"Not really." She shook her head,

glancing down so her twitching eye wouldn't be so noticeable. "What about you?" She approached the subject cautiously. "Did you catch lots of fish?"

"Only one."

"Did you bring it back? I can fry up a great trout."

Riley hated lying to her and pursed his lips. He swore that after this case he never would again. "I gave it to . . . a friend."

"I didn't think you had many friends in Portland." Her voice quavered slightly.

"I have plenty of friends." He raked his hand through his hair as he stalked to the other side of the room. He'd broken the cardinal rule in this business; the line between his professional life and his personal one had been crossed. He'd seen it happen to others and swore it wouldn't happen to him. But it was too late. He'd fallen for Jayne with his eyes wide open and wouldn't change a thing. "So, nothing new came up while I was away?"

Sheer nerve was the only thing that prevented Jayne from collapsing into a blubbering mass of tears. She wanted to shout at him not to lie to her — that she *knew.* Maybe not everything, but enough to doubt him, and it was killing her. She loved him, but she expected honesty. Their love would never last without it.

"While you were gone, I bought a dress for the reunion."

His eyes softened. "Can I see it?"

"I'd like to keep it a surprise."

Unable to help himself, he leaned

forward and pressed a lingering kiss to her lips. "That's fine, but you aren't going to surprise me with how beautiful you are. I've known that from the beginning."

Despite her efforts to the contrary, Jayne blushed. "You won't have any problem attending the reunion, will you?" If Riley was mixed up with Senator Priestly, then he probably wouldn't be able to leave the state.

Riley gave her an odd look. "No, why should I?"

"I don't know."

His eyebrows arched. "There's no problem, Jayne, and if there was, I'd do anything possible to deal with it." He wouldn't disappoint her. Not for the world. They were going to walk into that reunion together, and he was going to show her the time of her life.

The phone rang, and Jayne shrugged. "It's probably Gloria," she said as she hurried into the kitchen to answer it.

"I'm going down to collect my mail," Riley told her. "I'll be back in a minute."

"Okay."

Jayne was off the phone by the time Riley returned. He started to sort through a variety of envelopes, automatically tossing the majority of them. "What did Gloria have to say?" he asked with a preoccupied frown.

Jayne poured water into the coffeepot. "It . . . wasn't Gloria."

"Oh?" He raised his eyes to meet hers. "Who was it?"

"Mark Bauer." She had no reason

to feel guilty about Mark's call, but she did, incredibly so.

"Mark Bauer," Riley repeated, lowering his mail to the counter. "Has he made a habit of calling you since I've been gone?"

"No," she said. "Of course not."

Riley responded with a snort. He'd recognized Mark's type immediately. The guy wasn't all bad, just seeking a little companionship. The problem with Mark was that he had the mistaken notion that he was a lady-killer. He kept the lines of communication open with a dozen different women so that if one fell through there was always another. Only this time Mark had picked the wrong woman. Riley wasn't about to let that second-rate would-be player anywhere near Jayne.

"It's true, Riley," Jayne protested.

Mark hadn't contacted her in weeks.

"What did he want?"

"He suggested a movie next Saturday."

"And?"

"And I told him I wasn't interested."

"Good." Reassured, Riley resumed sorting through ten days' worth of junk mail.

"But . . . I'd go out with him if I wanted. It just so happens that I didn't feel like a movie, that's all." If he could lie to her so blithely, she could do the same. Jayne wouldn't have gone out with Mark again, but she didn't need to admit that to Riley.

Swiftly, she retreated into the living room, grabbing the remote and flicking on the TV, hoping to catch the evening news. If the early broadcast gave more details about the Max Priestly case, she could judge Riley's reaction to it.

Riley stiffened as he watched Jayne walk away, her spine straight and defiant. So she'd go out with other men if the mood struck her? Fine. "Go ahead," he announced.

Jayne turned around. "What do you mean?"

"You want to go out with other men, then do so with my blessing." Anger quivered in his voice. He didn't know what game Jayne was playing, but he wanted no part of it.

"I don't need your blessing."

"You're right. You don't." His teeth hurt from clenching them so tightly. "Listen, we're both tired. Let's call it a night. I'll talk to you in the morning."

"Fine." Primly, she crossed her arms and refused to meet his gaze.

But when the door closed, Jayne's confidence dissolved. Their meeting hadn't worked out the way she'd wanted. Instead of confronting Riley with what she'd learned, Jayne had tried to test his love.

After ten minutes of wearing a path in her carpet, Jayne decided that she was doomed to another sleepless night unless they settled this. She'd go to him and tell him she'd seen his car parked at Soft Sam's when he was supposedly fishing with friends. She'd also tell him she remembered seeing him and Senator Priestly in the apartment parking lot. Once she confronted Riley with the truth, he'd open up to her. And they were desperately in need of some honesty.

Standing outside his door, Jayne felt like a fool. Riley didn't answer her first tentative knock. She tried again, more loudly.

"Just a minute," she heard him shout.

Angrily Riley threw open the front door. His quickly donned bathrobe clung to his wet body. Droplets of water dripped from his wet hair.

"Jayne," he breathed, surprised to see her. "I was in the shower."

She stepped into the apartment, nervously clasping her hands. "Riley, I'm sorry about what I said earlier."

His smile brightened his dark face. "I know, love."

Awkwardly she began pacing. "We need to talk." They couldn't skirt the truth anymore. It had to come out, and it had to be now.

"Give me a minute to dress." He paused long enough to kiss her before disappearing into the bedroom.

Feeling a little out of place, Jayne moved into the living room. "Would you mind if I turned on the television?" she called out. The evening newscast could help her lead into the facts she'd unwittingly discovered.

"Sure, go ahead" came Riley's reply. "Remote's on top of the TV."

As she walked across the room, Jayne caught sight of a reddish leather briefcase sticking out from under the TV. She froze. This was the case she'd seen Senator Priestly hand over to Riley that afternoon so long ago. At least it appeared to be. She hadn't seen many of this color and this particular design.

Trembling, Jayne sank to her knees on the carpet and pulled out the briefcase. Her heart felt as though it was about to explode as she pressed open the two spring locks. The sound of the clasp opening seemed to reverberate around the room. For a panicked second she waited for Riley to rush in and demand to know what she was doing.

When nothing happened, Jayne pushed her glasses higher on her nose and carefully raised the lid. The briefcase was empty except for one file folder and one computer flash drive. Her heart pounding, Jayne opened the file. What she saw caused her breath to jam in her throat. She lifted the sheet that was a telephone log — Senator Priestly's calls. Sorting through the other papers, Jayne discovered copies of the incriminating letters that were said to be missing. Riley had in his possession the evidence necessary to convict Priestly. The very evidence that the police needed.

Feeling numb with shock and disbelief, Jayne quietly closed the case and returned it to its position under the TV.

She was sitting with her hands folded in her lap while Riley hummed cheerfully in the background. She couldn't confront Riley with what she'd found. At least not yet. Nor could she let him know what else she'd learned. If she was going to fall in love, why, oh why, did it have to be with a money-hungry felon?

Hurriedly Riley dressed, pleased that Jayne had come to him. He didn't understand why she'd started acting so silly. It was obvious that they were in love, and two people in love don't talk about dating others. His hands froze on his buttons. Maybe Jayne had seen him with Mimi again. No, he thought and expelled his breath. Jayne wouldn't have been able to hide it this well. He'd known almost instantly that there was something drastically wrong the first time she'd been upset. Something was bothering Jayne now, but it couldn't be anything as major as seeing him with that woman.

Walking into the living room, Riley paused. Jayne's spine was ramrod straight, and tears streamed down her ashen face.

"Jayne," he whispered. "What is it?"

She came to him then, linking her

arms around him. "I love you, Riley."

"I know, and I love you, too."

She sobbed once and buried her face in his shoulder.

"Honey, has someone hurt you?" he asked urgently.

She shook her head. "No." Breaking free, she wiped her cheeks. "I'm sorry. I'm being ridiculous. I . . . don't know what came over me." Immediately her right eye started twitching, and she stared down at the floor. "I just wanted to tell you I regret what happened earlier," she said in a low voice.

"I understand." But he didn't. Riley had never seen Jayne like this. "Are you hungry? Would you like to go out for dinner?" Showing himself in a public restaurant wouldn't be the smartest move, but they could find an out-of-the-way place.

"No," she said quickly, too quickly. "I'm not hungry. In fact, I've got this terrible headache. I should probably make it an early night."

Riley was skeptical. "If you want."

She backed away from him, inching toward the door. "Good night, Riley."

"Night, love. I'll see you in the morning."

Turning, she scurried across the room and out the door like a frightened mouse. More confused than ever, Riley rubbed his jaw. From the way Jayne was behaving, he could almost believe she knew something. But that was impossible. He'd gone to extreme measures to keep her out of this thing with Priestly.

Back inside her apartment, Jayne discovered that she couldn't stop shaking. The Riley Chambers she'd fallen in love with didn't seem to be the same man who'd returned from the fishing trip. Riley might believe he loved her, but secretly Jayne wondered how deep his love would be if he was aware of how much she knew.

Ignorance had been bliss, but her eyes were open now, and she had to take some kind of action. But *what* kind?

She'd refused to believe what the evidence told her about Riley; now she had to accept it. She didn't have any choice. No matter what the consequences, she had to act.

A sob escaped as she thought about that stupid class reunion, which had gotten her into this predicament in the first place. At this point, going back to St. Mary's was the last thing she wanted to do.

Tears squeezed past her tightly closed eyes, and Jayne gave up the effort to restrain them. She let them fall, needing the release they gave her. No one had ever told her that loving someone could be so painful. In all the books she'd read over the years, love had been a precious gift, something beyond price. Instead she'd found it to be painful, intense and ever so confusing.

Jayne didn't bother to go to bed. She sat in the darkened room, staring blankly at the walls, feeling wretched. More than wretched. The bitter disappointment cut through her. She didn't know what would happen to Riley once she talked to the police. If he hadn't already been arrested, they'd probably come for him after that.

Once again she entertained the idea of confronting him with what she'd discovered and asking him to do the honorable thing. And again she realized the impossibility of that request. Riley had lied to her several times. She couldn't trust him. And yet, she still loved him. . . .

As the sky lightened with early morning, Jayne noticed that the clouds were heavy and gray. It seemed like an omen, a premonition of what was to come.

Knowing what she had to do, Jayne waited until she guessed Riley was awake before phoning him.

"I won't be going to work today," she told him, unable to keep the anguish out of her voice.

Riley hesitated. It sounded as if

Jayne was ready to burst into tears. "Jayne," he said, unsure of how much to pressure her right now, "honey, tell me what's wrong."

"I've . . . still got this horrible headache," she said on a rush of emotion. "I'm fine, really. Don't worry about me. And, Riley, I want you to know something important."

"What is it?" Momentarily he tensed.

"I care about you. I'll probably never love anyone more than I love you."

"Jayne . . ."

"I've got to call the library and tell them I won't be in."

"I'll talk to you this evening."

"Okay," she said hoarsely.

Ten minutes later, she heard him leave. She waited another fifteen and made two brief phone calls. One to Gloria at the library and another to a local cab company, requesting a taxi.

The cab arrived in a few minutes, and Jayne walked out of the lobby and into the car.

"Where to, miss?" the balding driver asked.

She reached for a fresh tissue. She hadn't put on her glasses because she kept having to take them off to mop up the tears. "The downtown police station," she whispered, hardly recognizing her own voice. "And hurry, please."

NINE

Lieutenant Hal Powers brought Jayne a cup of coffee and sat down at the table across from her. She supposed this little room was normally used for the interrogation of suspects. This morning she felt like a criminal herself, reporting the man she loved to the police.

"Now, Ms. Gilbert, would you like to start again?"

"I'm sorry," she murmured, brushing away the tears. "I told myself I wouldn't get emotional, and then I end up like this."

Lieutenant Powers gave her an encouraging smile. Jayne had liked him immediately. He was a sensitive man, and she hadn't expected that. From various mysteries she'd read, Jayne had assumed that the police often became cynical and callous. Lieutenant Powers displayed neither of those characteristics.

She gripped the foam cup with both hands and stared into it blindly. "I live in the Marlia Apartments, and I . . . have this neighbor. I suspect he may be involved in something that could get him into a great deal of trouble."

"What has your neighbor been doing?" the lieutenant asked gently.

"I think highly of this neighbor, and I . . . I don't want to say anything until I know what would happen to him."

Lieutenant Powers frowned. "That depends on what he's done."

Jayne took another sip of coffee in an effort to stall for time and clear her thoughts. "To be honest, I can't say for sure that . . . my neighbor's done anything unlawful. But he's holding something that he shouldn't. Something of value."

"Does it belong to him?"

Jayne's eyes fell to the smooth table-top. "Not exactly."

"Do you know who it does belong to?"

With dismay in her heart, she nodded.

"Who?"

Jayne was silent. There'd never been a darker moment in her life.

"Ms. Gilbert?"

"What I found," she said as tears once again crept down the side of her face, "belongs to Senator Max Priestly."

The lieutenant straightened. "Do you know how your neighbor got this — whatever it is?"

"It's a briefcase with telephone logs and incriminating letters." Now that she'd finally spilled it out, she didn't feel any better. In fact, she felt worse.

"How did your neighbor get this briefcase?"

"I saw the senator give it to Ril— my neighbor." She hurried on to add, "He, my neighbor, doesn't realize that I saw the exchange or that I know what's inside."

"How *do* you know?"

Jayne's gaze locked with his. "I looked."

"I see." The lieutenant rose and walked to the other side of the room. "Ms. Gilbert —"

"Could you tell me what will happen to him?"

One side of his mouth lifted in a half smile. "I'm not sure. . . ." He appeared preoccupied as he moved toward the door. "Could you excuse me for a minute?"

"Of course."

Lieutenant Powers left the room, and Jayne covered her face with both hands. This was so much worse than she'd imagined. Her deepest fear was that the police would insist she lead them to Riley. She felt enough like an informer. A betrayer . . . If only she'd been able to talk to Riley, confront him — but that would've been impossible. Loving him the way she did, she would've been eager to believe anything he told her. Jayne couldn't trust herself around Riley. So she'd done the unthinkable. She'd gone to the police to turn in the only man she'd ever loved.

The door opened, and Lieutenant Powers returned. "I think you two have something you need to discuss."

Jayne suddenly noticed that the lieutenant wasn't alone. Behind him stood Riley.

Jayne's mouth sagged open in utter disbelief.

"I'll wait for you outside," Powers added.

"Thanks, Hal," Riley said as the lieutenant walked out the door.

"Oh, Riley!" Jayne leapt to her feet. "I'm so sorry I had to do this!" she cried through her tears.

"Jayne . . ."

"No." She held up her hand to stop him. "Please, don't say anything. Just listen. I told you this morning that I love you, and I meant that with all my heart. We're going to get through this together. I promise you that I'll be by your side no matter how long you're in prison. I'll come and visit you and write every day until . . . until you're free again. You can turn your life around if you want. I believe in you." She spoke with all the fervency of her love.

Riley's mouth narrowed into a hard line.

"You told me once that you wanted to change," Jayne reminded him. "Let me help you. I want to do everything I can."

"Jayne —"

Her hand gripped his. "Riley, I beg you, please, please tell them everything."

He pulled his hand free. "Jayne, honestly, would you stop being so melodramatic!"

Melodramatic? She blinked, unsure that she'd heard him correctly. "What do you mean?"

"There's no need for you to write me in prison."

"But . . ."

"Jayne, I'm with the FBI. I've been working undercover for six months." Witnessing her distress, Riley cursed himself for not having told her sooner. He also realized that he *couldn't* have told her. Doing so could have put the entire operation in jeopardy. Breaking cover went against everything that had been ingrained in him from the time he was a rookie. But seeing the anguish Jayne had suffered was enough to persuade him that he had to explain.

"Honey, I couldn't tell you."

Stunned, Jayne managed to nod.

"I would've put you in danger if I had."

She continued staring at him. Riley, her Riley, worked for the FBI. She waited for the surge of relief to fill her. None came.

"Why do you have the evidence needed to convict Senator Priestly?" Her voice sounded frail and quavering.

"I'm working undercover, Jayne. I can't really say any more than that."

She didn't understand what being undercover had to do with anything. Then it dawned on her. "You're trying to catch someone else?"

Riley nodded.

"Doesn't that put you in a dangerous position?"

He shrugged nonchalantly. "It could."

Hal Powers stuck his head inside the door. "You two got everything straightened out yet?"

"Not quite," Riley answered for them.

"You want a refill on that coffee?" Powers asked Jayne.

She looked down at the half-full cup. "No, thanks."

"What about you, Riley?"

Riley shook his head, but Jayne noticed the look of respect and admiration the other man gave him.

"This isn't the first time you've done something like this, is it?" she asked.

"She doesn't know about Boston?" Hal stepped into the room, his voice enthusiastic. He paused to glance at Riley. "You've got yourself a famous neighbor, Ms. Gilbert. We even heard about that case out here. Folks call it the second French Connection."

Riley didn't look pleased to have the lieutenant reveal quite so much about his past.

"If you're working undercover, what are you doing here, in the police station?"

"He came to talk to you," Powers inserted.

Riley tossed him an angry glare. "I said I wasn't interested in coffee," he stated flatly.

Powers didn't have to be told twice. "Sure. If you need me, give me a call."

"Right." Riley crossed the room and closed the door behind the other man.

Given a moment's respite Jayne blew her nose and stuffed the tissue inside her purse. Her hand shook as she secured the clasp. She'd made a complete fool of herself.

"How did you know about the briefcase?" Riley asked, turning back to her.

"You were careless, Riley," she said in a small voice. "The corner was poking out from under your TV."

Riley didn't bother to correct her. The briefcase was exactly where it was supposed to be.

"What made you check the contents?" Jayne wasn't the meddling type. She must have suspected something to have taken it upon herself to peek inside that briefcase.

"I saw Max Priestly give it to you weeks ago . . . before I knew you. It was late one Saturday afternoon, in the parking lot."

Riley frowned. "Since you seem to have figured out that much, you're probably aware that my fishing trip —"

She gave a tiny half sob, half laugh. "I know. You don't need to explain."

Riley doubted she really knew, but he wasn't at liberty to elaborate. "I didn't want to lie to you. When this is over, I'll never do it again."

Jayne stood up. All she wanted to do now was escape. "I was obtuse. If I hadn't been so melodramatic, as you put it, I would have guessed sooner."

"You did the right thing. I know how difficult coming here must have been."

Jayne didn't deny it. She was sure there'd never be anything more physically or mentally draining — except telling Riley goodbye. Her hand tightened around the strap of her purse as she prepared to leave. "I . . ."

"Let's get out of here." Riley took her hand and raised it to his lips. "I'm sorry for having put you through this."

She quickly shook her head. "I put myself through it."

"We're done in here," Riley told Lieutenant Powers on the way out the door. He slipped his arm around Jayne's waist. "Where do you want me to drop you off?"

"But . . . you don't want to be seen

coming out of here, do you?"

"Having you with me would make an explanation easier if the wrong person happens to see me. Do you want to go home?"

"Yes, please. I didn't sleep well last night."

Again Riley felt the bitterness of regret. Unwittingly he'd involved Jayne in this situation and put her through emotional distress. Once he was through with the Priestly case, he planned to accept a management position in law enforcement and work at a desk. He'd had enough risk and subterfuge. More than enough. He wanted Jayne as his wife, and he wanted children. He pictured a son and daughter and felt an emotion so strong that it seemed as though his heart had constricted. Jayne was everything honest and good, and he desperately needed her in his life.

The ride back to the apartment building was completed in silence. Although she'd been awake all the night, Jayne didn't think she'd be able to sleep now. Her mind had shifted into double time, spinning furiously as she sorted through the facts she'd recently learned.

When Riley parked the car and walked her into the building, Jayne was mildly surprised. She hadn't expected him to be so solicitous. Besides, she'd prefer to be alone, for the next few hours anyway.

She paused outside her apartment door, not wanting him to come in. "I'm fine. You don't have to stay."

She didn't look fine. In fact, he couldn't remember ever seeing her this pale. "Do you need an aspirin?" he asked, following her inside.

"No." Jayne couldn't believe that he hadn't noticed her lack of welcome. Too much had happened, and she needed time alone to find her place in the scheme of things — if she had a place. Everything was different now. Nothing about her relationship with Riley would remain the same.

"There's aspirin in my apartment if you need some."

"I'm fine," she said again. "Really."

He helped her out of her jacket and glanced at the heap of discarded tissues on the coffee table. The evidence that Jayne had spent a sleepless night crying lay before him. "Honey, why didn't you say something when you found the briefcase?"

She shrugged, not answering.

"You must've been frantic." He picked up the wadded tissues and dumped them in the kitchen garbage. The fact that Jayne had left a mess in her neatly organized apartment told him how great her distress had been. Riley wanted to kick himself for having put her through this.

"I was a little worried," was all she'd admit.

"I can't understand why you wouldn't confront me with what you knew." He'd raised his voice, but his irritation was directed more at himself than at Jayne. Riley didn't know what his response would have been had she come to him, but at least he could have prevented this night of anxious tears.

"I couldn't!" she cried angrily. She pulled another tissue from the box.

Riley frowned tiredly. "Why not?"

"It's obvious that you don't know anything about love," she said sharply. "When you love someone, it's so easy to believe the excuses he or she gives you — because you want to trust that person so badly. You've lied to me repeatedly, Riley. . . . You've had to. I understand that now. But . . . but —" She paused to inhale a deep breath. "I couldn't tell you *before* I knew that. I couldn't have counted on you telling me the truth, and worse, I couldn't have trusted my own response."

"Oh, my love." Riley wrapped her in his arms, fully appreciating her dilemma for the first time.

The pressure of his hands molded her against him, and her hands slipped around his neck. Her pulse thundered in her ears when he raised her chin and then she felt the warmth of his mouth on hers. His kiss melted away the frost that had enclosed her heart.

When the kiss was over, Jayne reeled slightly. His hands steadied her. "I've got to get back," he said.

She took a step away from him, breaking all physical contact, trying to put distance between them. It was far too easy to fall into his arms and accept the comfort of his kiss. "I understand. Don't worry about me, Riley. I'll go to bed and probably sleep all day." At least she hoped she would, but something told her differently.

"I'll call you this afternoon."

"Okay," she told him and walked him to the door. He kissed her again briefly and was gone.

Standing in the hallway, Riley felt like ramming his fist through the wall. He would've given anything to have avoided this. She looked so small and lost, her face drained, her expression shocked. He'd thought Priestly and his accomplice would've made their move by now. He'd been waiting days for this thing to be over. Jayne's reunion was this coming weekend; he'd make sure all the loose ends were tied up by then.

Putting on her glasses, Jayne wandered over to the living room window and watched from nine floors above as Riley, carrying the briefcase, approached his car. He got in and pulled out of the lot and onto the street. Still standing at the window, Jayne saw another car pull out almost immediately after and follow him. Her heart jumped into her throat when she realized that he was being tailed.

Craning her neck, she saw the blue sedan behind him turn at the same intersection. Nervously she rubbed her palms together, wondering what she should do. She had no way of contacting Riley. The only phone number she had was for his apartment, not his cell.

Running into the kitchen, she called the police and asked for Lieutenant Powers, saying it was an emergency.

"Powers here," she heard a moment later.

"Lieutenant," Jayne said, fighting down her panic. "This is Jayne Gilbert. Riley dropped me off at my apartment, and I saw someone follow him."

"Listen, Ms. Gilbert, I wouldn't worry. Riley's been working under-cover a lot of years. He can take care of himself."

"But . . ."

"I doubt anyone would tail Riley Chambers without him knowing about it."

"But he's concerned about me. He may not be paying attention the way he should. Could you please contact him and let him know?" She raised her voice, trying to impress the ur-gency of her request on him.

"Ms. Gilbert, I don't think —"

"Riley's life could be in danger!"

She could hear the lieutenant's sigh of resignation. "If it'll reassure you, then I'll contact him."

"Thank you." But Jayne wasn't

completely mollified; she was also worried about how Riley would react. He wouldn't appreciate her warning. He might even be insulted. As Powers had claimed, Riley had been around a long time. He knew how to take care of himself.

Sagging onto the sofa, Jayne found that her knees were trembling. She couldn't help imagining Riley caught in a trap from which he couldn't escape. Forcefully she dispelled the images from her mind. This wasn't Riley's first case, she reminded herself, and it probably wouldn't be his last. That knowledge wasn't comforting. Not in the least. Loving Riley Chambers wasn't going to work. Could he really change the way he lived? He'd tasted adventure, lived with excitement; a house with a white picket fence would be so mundane to someone like him.

Jayne woke hours later, shocked that she'd managed to sleep. She rubbed a hand along the back of her neck to ease the crick she'd gotten from sleeping with her head propped against the sofa arm. Brilliant sunlight splashed in through her open drapes, and a glance at her watch said it was after five. She suddenly realized that Riley hadn't called. She wouldn't have slept through the ringing of the phone.

Pushing the hair away from her face, she swallowed down the fear that threatened to overtake her. Fleetingly she wondered if Powers had warned him about the blue sedan. She doubted it. It was obvious from their conversation that the lieutenant thought she was overreacting. Maybe she was.

In an effort to calm her fears, Jayne looked out her window. His parking space was empty, she noted sadly, and then felt a surge of relief when his car made a left-hand turn a block away. She also took consolation from the knowledge that there wasn't a blue car anywhere near Riley's.

But her relief quickly died when Jayne noticed a blue sedan parked on the side street. It might not have been the same one, but the resemblance was close enough to alarm her. Jayne was undecided — should she do anything? — until she saw a man climb out of the car. He paused and looked both ways before crossing the street to head in Riley's direction.

Jayne's heart flew into her throat

when she watched him step behind a parked car, apparently to wait. It occurred to her that he could be planning to ambush Riley. Instantly she knew she was right. Jayne could sense it, could feel the threat. She had to get to Riley and warn him.

Without another thought, she raced out of her apartment and down the hall. For once, the elevator appeared immediately. By the time the wide doors opened into the lobby, Jayne was frantic.

She ran outside and came to an abrupt halt. She couldn't run up to Riley. She might be putting him in even greater danger if she intervened now. The thing to do was remain calm and see what the man planned to do — if anything.

Walking into the lot, Jayne saw Riley standing beside his car with the briefcase. He wasn't moving. The other man faced him and had his back to her. Approaching the pair at an angle, Jayne caught a flash of metal. The man had a gun trained on Riley.

Tension momentarily froze her, but she knew what she had to do. She broke into a run.

Riley saw her move, and terror burned through him. A scream rose in his throat as he called out, "Jayne . . . no!"

TEN

Jayne saw the way Riley's face had become drawn and white as she'd started to run. She didn't know much about martial arts, but after the incident with the mugger, she'd read a wonderfully simple book filled with illustrations. When she'd finished the book, Jayne had felt fairly confident that she could defend herself, if need be. Seeing a gun pointed at Riley's heart was all the incentive she needed to apply the lessons she'd learned.

Unfortunately her skill wasn't quite up to what she'd hoped it would be, and her aim fell far below his chest, possibly because she wasn't wearing her glasses. But where her foot struck caused enough pain to double the man over and send him slumping to the pavement. The gun went flying.

Riley recovered it. His face was pinched and drawn. "For crying out loud, Jayne. I don't believe you." He rubbed a hand over his face. "You idiot! Couldn't you see he had a gun?"

Feeling undeniably proud of herself, Jayne smiled shyly. "Of course I saw the gun."

"Did it ever occur to you that you might've been shot?" he shouted.

She shrugged. "To be honest, I didn't really think of that. I just . . . acted."

The man she'd felled remained on

the ground, moaning. From seemingly nowhere, a uniformed officer appeared and forced him to stand before handcuffing his wrists.

Riley paced back and forth, and for the first time Jayne noticed how furious he was. The self-satisfied grin faded from her face. The least Riley could do was show a little appreciation. "I saved your life, for heaven's sake."

"Saved it?" He shook his head, momentarily closing his eyes. "You nearly cost us both our lives."

"But . . ."

"Do you think I'm stupid? I knew that Simpson — Priestly's campaign manager and accomplice — was in the parking lot. We were surrounded by three teams of plainclothes detectives. In addition, a squad car was parked on the other side of the building."

"Oh," Jayne replied in a small voice.

"You scared me half to death." He groaned. "And you're the one who hides her eyes during movies." He raked his fingers through his hair. "How do you think I'd feel if something happened to you?" Some of the harsh anger drained from his voice.

"I did what I thought I had to," Jayne returned, feeling faintly indignant.

Riley shook his head again. "I don't think my system could take another one of your acts of heroism. Where did you learn to leap through the air like that?"

"In a book . . ."

"You mean to tell me you learned that crippling move from something you read?"

"The illustrations were excellent, but I have to admit I was off a bit. I was actually aiming for his chest."

Riley just rolled his eyes.

"Under the circumstances," she said, trying to maintain her dignity, "I thought I did rather well."

Briefly his gaze met hers, and a reluctant grin lifted his mouth. "You did fine, but promise me you'll never, *ever* interfere again."

"I promise." Now that everything was over, reaction set in, and Jayne began to tremble. She'd seen Riley in terrible danger and responded without a thought for her own welfare. Riley was as incredulous as the policemen who milled around, shaking their heads in wonder at this woman who'd downed an armed man.

"Are you all right?" he asked, draping an arm around her shoulders and pulling her close. He savored the warmth of her body next to his.

"I'm fine." She wasn't, but she couldn't very well break down now.

"I've got to go downtown and debrief, write my report. But I'll be back in a couple of hours. Will you be all right until I return?"

"Of course."

Riley hesitated. Jayne was putting on a brave front, but he could tell that she was frightened now that she'd realized what could have happened. He didn't want to leave her, but it was unavoidable.

"I'll walk you to your apartment," he said, wanting to reassure her that everything was under control.

"I'm fine," she insisted in a shaky

voice. "You're needed at the station."

"Jayne," he said, then paused.

"Go on," she urged. "I'll be waiting here. I'm not going anyplace."

He dropped a quick kiss on her mouth. "I love you, Jayne." And he did love her — so much that he doubted he could have survived if anything had happened to her.

As he left, Jayne went back to her apartment, telling herself Riley was safe, and that was what mattered most.

An hour later, Jayne reached her decision. It wasn't so difficult, really. She'd known it would come to this sooner or later, and she'd prefer it to be sooner. Again, as she had in the parking lot, she was only doing what she had to.

By the time Riley appeared, she was

composed and confident. She opened her door and stepped aside as he entered her apartment. He bent to kiss her, and she let him, savoring the moment.

"We need to talk." She spoke first, not giving him a chance to say anything.

"You're telling me," Riley said with a grin. "I still can't get over you." If he lived for another century, Riley doubted he would forget those few seconds when Jayne had come running toward Simpson. And she'd done it to protect *him* — Riley Chambers. Naturally, she'd been unaware that he wasn't in any danger. All the way back from the jail, Riley was lost in the memory of those brief moments. He'd found himself an exceptional woman. And he wasn't going to lose her. He'd already started looking at diamond rings. On the night of her reunion he was going to ask her to marry him.

"Riley, about the reunion."

"What about it?"

"I've asked Mark to take me."

"What?"

"I want you to know I appreciate the fact that you were willing to attend it with me, but —"

"Jayne, you're not thinking straight," Riley countered, still not believing what she'd said.

She forced out a light laugh. "Actually, I've been giving it some thought over the past few days. This wasn't a sudden decision. When I went to the police this morning, I knew there was every likelihood that you wouldn't be able to go to Seattle with me."

Riley frowned. "So you asked Mark?"

"Yes." Her right eye remained still. Riley had taught her several things, and one of those was how to lie. The smoothness with which she told him this one was shocking. What a sad commentary on their relationship, Jayne mused unhappily. She'd love Riley forever, and years from now, when the hurt went away, she'd be able to look back on their weeks together and be glad she'd known and loved him — however briefly.

Riley clenched his fists. "Something's not right here. You're lying."

"I'm not the expert in that department. You are." She stalked into the kitchen. "Here," she said, handing him the telephone receiver. "If you don't believe me, call Mark."

Riley stared at the phone in utter astonishment. "Jayne . . . don't do this." His gut instinct told him she was lying.

"How was I supposed to know you weren't some crook? I couldn't take that chance. So . . . I asked Mark."

"Then unask him."

"I won't do that."

"Why not?" Riley was becoming angrier with every breath.

"Because I'm not sure you're the type of man I'd want to go with — the type of man I want to be with." The pain of what she was doing was so powerful that Jayne reached out to hold on to the kitchen counter. "I'm sorry, Riley, I am. I've known for some time that things weren't working out."

"Not sorry enough." Abruptly he

swiveled around. "I'd suggest you have fun, but I doubt you will with Mark Bauer."

"I'm sure I'll have a perfectly good time," she lied, but the effort to hold back her tears made the words unintelligible.

"Jayne, darling, let me look at you." Dorothy Gilbert held her daughter by the shoulders and shook her gray head. Jayne's parents had met her at the train station. "You look fabulous."

Jayne smiled absently. The train had arrived on time. She was afraid to fly, but she beamed proudly at the thought of the one shining moment in her life when she'd ignored her fear and attacked a gunman. Such ironies were common with her.

"The new hairstyle suits you."

"Thank you, Mom." But the happiness she felt at seeing her parents didn't compensate for the emptiness inside her after that last confrontation with Riley. From her mother's arm, Jayne moved forward to receive her father's gruff embrace.

"Good to see you, sweetie," Howard Gilbert said.

"Thank you, Daddy."

Slowly they walked toward the terminal where Jayne was to collect her luggage.

"That Thomas girl arrived this morning from California. You might want to call her at her parents' house," Dorothy told Jayne as she put an arm around her waist. "She's already called to ask about you."

"I . . . I'd like to talk to her."

"She's married and has two daughters."

"How nice." Jayne wasn't married. Nor did she have children. She was the prim and proper woman Riley had accused her of being. It was what she'd been destined to be from the time she'd graduated from high school. She had been a fool to believe otherwise. Angry with herself for the self-pitying thoughts, Jayne smiled brightly at her mother.

"Judy said the reception at the Westin starts about eight."

"They mailed me a program, Mom." Jayne had decided she'd attend the reunion alone. Her dream had been to arrive with Riley at her side, but that was out of the question. So, as she'd done most of her life, Jayne would pretend. She'd walk into the reception with her head held high and imagine everyone turning toward her and sighing with envy.

She hadn't seen Riley. Not once since that fateful afternoon. For all she knew he could have moved out of the building. She was grateful he'd accepted her lies, making it unnecessary to fabricate others. She'd purposely hurt him to be kind. She wasn't the right woman for him, and his life was too different from hers.

She'd read about the charges against Priestly and Simpson. The articles and news reports gave an abbreviated version of Riley's part in all this, mentioning only that an FBI agent had worked with police departments statewide to destroy Priestly's organization.

Her father collected her suitcase, and then the three of them walked to the car parked across from the King Street Station.

"I have a lovely new dress," Jayne said.

"I'm so pleased you're attending this reunion, Jayne. I'd been worried you might not want to go." She stared intently at Jayne.

"I wouldn't miss it, Mom."

"Those girls never appreciated you," her father commented, placing Jayne's suitcase in the trunk of the car.

"Nonsense, Dad, I had some good friends."

"She did, Howard."

They chatted companionably on the drive toward Jayne's childhood home on Queen Anne Hill.

Once she got home, Jayne phoned her high school friend, Judy Thomas, and they chatted for nearly an hour.

"It's so good to talk to you again," Judy said. "I can hardly wait to see you."

"Me, too."

"I think I'd better get off the phone. Dad's giving me disapproving looks just like he did ten years ago."

"I guess we'll always be teenagers to our parents."

"Unfortunately." Judy giggled.

Jayne smiled when her mother stuck her head around the corner. "Don't you think you should start to get ready?"

Jayne contained a smile. Judy was right. They would always be teenagers to their parents. "Okay, Mom, I'll be off in a minute."

"See what I mean?" Judy said.

"Oh, yes. Listen, I'll see you tonight."

"See you then."

Jayne spent most of the next hour preparing for the reunion. Her mother raved about how the dress looked on Jayne. Gazing at her mirrored reflection, Jayne's astonishment was renewed. The dress was the most beautiful one she'd ever owned.

Adding the final touches to her makeup, Jayne heard her mother and father whispering in the background.

"We'd like to get some pictures of you and your young man," her father said when Jayne stepped out of her bedroom.

"Pardon me, Dad?"

"Pictures," he repeated, taking his camera from the case. "Go stand by the fireplace."

"All right." She went into the living

room and stopped cold. Before her stood Riley. Tall, polished, impeccable and so incredibly good-looking in his tuxedo that she felt as though all the oxygen had escaped her lungs.

"Riley . . . what are you doing here?"

"Taking you to the reunion."

"But how did you know —"

"I believe your father wants to take a few pictures." Gently he took her lifeless hand in his and tucked it into his elbow.

Smiling, Dorothy and Howard Gilbert moved into the living room.

"Oh — Mom and Dad, this is Riley Chambers."

Riley came forward and shook hands with her parents. "Glad to see you again, Howard. And good to meet you, Dorothy."

Gruffly, her father motioned for the couple to stand in front of the fireplace while he took a series of photos.

"I believe these young people need a few minutes alone."

"Daddy —"

"You need to talk to your fiancé," Howard said, taking his wife by the arm and leading her into the kitchen.

Jayne didn't move and barely breathed, and she couldn't seem to speak.

"Having her father announce it isn't the most romantic way to tell the woman you love that you want to marry her," Riley said once her parents had left.

"Oh, Riley, please don't."

"Don't what? Love you? That would be impossible."

"No," she whispered miserably,

hanging her head. "Don't ask me."

"But I am. Maybe it was presumptuous of me, but I bought a ring." He pulled out a jeweler's box from his inside pocket. "I don't know why you lied about inviting Mark. I don't even care. I love you, and we're going to have a marvelous life together."

"Riley." She swallowed a sob. "No, I won't marry you."

He put the jeweler's box on the mantel behind him and stared at her, his look incredulous. "Why?"

"Because I'm me. I'll never be anything other than a children's librarian. That's all I've ever wanted to be. You live life in the fast lane, while I crawl along at a snail's pace — if you'll forgive the clichés."

"But, Jayne, I'm sick of that life . . ."

"For how long? A year? Maybe

two?"

"Jayne, I've already accepted a job — a desk job — with the Portland police. My undercover days are over."

"Riley, are you sure that's what you want?"

"I've never been more sure of anything." His eyes held a determination that few would challenge. "I've waited half my life for you, Jayne Gilbert, and I'm not taking no for an answer."

The blunt words took Jayne aback. Her lips tightened as she shook her head.

"Do you love me so little?" he asked in a voice that was so soft she could hardly hear it.

"You know I love you!" she cried.

"Then why are you fighting me?"

"I'm . . . afraid, Riley."

He took a step toward her, extending his hand. "Then put your hand in mine. No man could ever love you more than I do. I'm ready for everything you have to give me. I've been ready for a lot of years."

Jayne couldn't fight him anymore. Tentatively, she raised her hand and placed it in his.

"I believe we have a reunion to attend."

"It isn't necessary. You know that, don't you? All I've ever needed is you." She blinked back tears. "Now, don't make me cry. It took me ages to get this makeup right."

"You're beautiful."

She laughed and reached up to kiss him. "Thank you, but I have trouble believing that."

"After tonight, you won't. I'll be the

envy of every man there."

"Then it's true," Jayne said with a trembling smile. "Love is blind."

Riley turned to retrieve the jeweler's box and offered it to her. Smiling tremulously, she let him slide the engagement ring on her finger.

"What would you say to a fall wedding?"

Before Jayne could respond, Howard and Dorothy reappeared, and Dorothy protested, "Oh, no, that's nowhere near enough time!"

"It's fine, Dorothy," Howard said. "The only thing that matters to me is whether our daughter's marrying the right man. And I'm convinced she couldn't find anyone better than Riley." He winked at his wife. "I know you, of all people, can pull off a wedding in four months."

Dorothy gave a resigned sigh. "Have fun, you two," she murmured.

"We will, Mom."

On the way down the sidewalk to Riley's parked car, Jayne gave him an odd look. "When did you talk to my father?"

"A couple of days ago when I asked his permission for his daughter's hand."

"Riley, you didn't!"

He raised his eyebrows. "I did. I told you before that I was going to do everything right with you. We're going to be married as soon as possible — in a church before God and witnesses. We're going to be very happy, Jayne."

A brilliant smile curved her lips. "I think we will, too," she said.

A half-hour later, Riley pulled into

the curved driveway of the downtown Westin where the reunion was being held. He eased to a stop, and an attendant opened Jayne's door and helped her out.

They walked through the hotel lobby and took the elevator to the Grand Ballroom.

"Ready?" Riley asked as they approached.

Her breath felt tight in her lungs. "I think so."

One step into the room, and Jayne felt every eye on her. The room went silent as she turned and smiled into the warmth and love that radiated from Riley's gaze.

Whispers rose. And the girls of St. Mary's sighed.

The employees of Thorndike Press hope you have enjoyed this Large Print book. All our Thorndike, Wheeler, and Kennebec Large Print titles are designed for easy reading, and all our books are made to last. Other Thorndike Press Large Print books are available at your library, through selected bookstores, or directly from us.

For information about titles, please call:
  (800) 223-1244

or visit our Web site at:
  http://gale.cengage.com/thorndike

To share your comments, please write:
  Publisher
  Thorndike Press
  10 Water St., Suite 310
  Waterville, ME 04901